SPASM ROCKERS

JAMISON

NIQUEL

JAMISON
Copyright © 2016 Niquel
All rights reserved.

ISBN: 978–0-9961492–4-2 (eBook)
ISBN: 978–0-9961492–5-9 (paperback)

Editor: Kiezha Ferrell, Librum Artis Editorial Services,
www.facebook.com/librumartis
Editor: Carol, The Blurb Bitch,
www.facebook.com/The-BLURB-BITCH-979103745473050/
Interior Designer: Tami, Integrity Formatting,
www.facebook.com/IntegrityFormatting/
Proofreader: Judy, www.facebook.com/judysproofreading

Dedication

To my girls,
you were the first ones to know about Jamison, and loved him before I even finished the story. I couldn't do this without your support, mommy loves you!

To my family,
who have been behind me since my first book and never thought I was crazy for making up these steamy stories!

To Grandpa,
thanks for letting Jamison share your birthday!

And lastly, this is dedicated to you, reader.
If it wasn't for your kind messages, your reviews, and your support, I wouldn't be where I am today. Thank you!

Chapter 1

Eleven years earlier

"Oh my God, Shan, quit being a wuss!"

"I can't, it's too high!" I yelled down at my brother, who was safe on the ground. I don't know why I let him talk me into doing stupid things like this.

"C'mon, Shanny, just put your foot in the holes and jump when you get to the last one," CJ egged on.

Anytime he was around and asked me to do something, the fear inside of me went away. "Okay."

One.

Two.

Three.

"Ouch!"

"Holy crap, are you all right?" my brother asked, as the sky spun behind his and CJ's heads.

"My head hurts really bad."

"Dang, I'll go and get Mom. Can you stay with her, CJ?" He nodded his head, and then helped me sit up. He kept looking at me funny with his eyes; eyes that were the color of chocolate.

"Why are you looking at me like that?"

"I was looking at the small dots across your face. What are they?"

I placed my hands over my face, and rubbed my cheeks, wishing they would come off. "My mommy calls them 'freckles' and I hate them."

"Why?"

"Because people are always teasing me about them. Mom said I got them from being in the sun too much."

"So let's call them sun kisses! The sun loved your face so much, it left little kisses behind."

I giggled so hard, that it made my head hurt more. CJ was almost thirteen, like my older brother, but he made me feel fuzzy inside.

"Shannon Marie Moore, what happened? Oh my Lord, you're bleeding! Ambrose Dean Moore, I'm going to kill you!"

"It wasn't even my fault this time, Mom!" he yelled.

After a few painful stitches in the back of my head, Mom took me to get some ice cream before bringing us all back home. The boys didn't get any since it was their fault I fell. I made sure I rubbed that in Amby's face.

"You three can sit on the porch until dinner is ready. No more climbing trees!" Mom yelled.

"I'm really sorry, Shan," CJ said as he put his arm around my shoulders.

"It's okay. I shouldn't have gone up that high, I never did that before."

"Shan, you're going to do it again, and next time you won't fall. If you do, I'll rip Mr. Snuffles' head off."

Mr. Snuffles was my favorite stuffed elephant, and I brought him everywhere with me. "I hate you, Amby."

"I hate you more."

CJ had been at our house so much lately that I began to wonder if his parents even cared about him. I'd only seen his mom and dad a few times, but most of the time my mom and dad took care of him.

I don't know what was happening to me lately, but the more we all hung out, the more I liked him. He was so cute. His brown hair was really short, he was taller than me, and wore jeans and different t-shirts with band names on them. His favorite group out of all of them was Metallica.

"Dean, what are you doing for your birthday next week?" CJ asked. He always called my brother by his middle name because it sounded cooler.

"I don't know, but I asked Mom for a monster truck theme. Turning thirteen is a big freakin' deal, and I don't want any more kiddie-themed parties." He rolled his eyes at me when he said that.

"What? I'm not a kid. I love cartoons, so what!"

"You're nine, poop face. It's okay for *you* to have kiddie parties."

"Whatever."

Chapter 2

It was my best friend, Dean's, birthday, and I was so excited. Mom and Dad gave me enough money to buy him this really cool monster truck, and I made sure no one else was going to get the same thing. I knew he was gonna freakin' flip when he saw it. It was huge, red, which is his favorite color, and it had big wheels on it with real tread. It was voice-controlled and came with its own rechargeable batteries. I almost wanted to keep it for myself.

"Have fun at the party, Cody!" Mom said as I finished taping up the present. She'd taken the day off from work as a waitress and looked like she was really sad for some reason. I didn't have enough time to ask her what was wrong because I had to get to the party and help Mrs. Moore set up.

"Mom, I hope you're okay."

"I am, sweetie. We'll talk when you get home later."

"Mom, I'm staying the night over there, remember?"

"Oh—that's right, sorry, love. Have a good time and we'll talk tomorrow sometime. I love you."

I raised my eyebrow at her, confused, but grabbed my overnight bag, tossed my present inside and ran out the door to the party.

I darted inside the Moores' house and handed my present to Shan before I ran upstairs with my bag. Shannon looked very nice today, with her hair brushed back into a braid and a new floral dress.

I opened the door and saw Dean sitting on the side of his bed. "What's wrong, bro?"

"I asked Sally Jenson to come to my party."

"Do you think she'll show up?"

"Who knows, but I really like her. I was hoping to have my first kiss with her."

"Wow. I'm sure she'll be here." What he didn't know was, I had already talked to her and she liked him too. She told me she would come and for me to act surprised when she showed up. Dean didn't do well with secrets, but I'd tell him I knew about it later.

"Cody, Ambrose, come on down. I want to take a picture of you guys with Shannon before the party starts."

"Coming, Mom!"

I wore my favorite AC/DC shirt underneath the ugly plaid shirt my mom made me wear for the party. As soon as it was over, I was going to rip it off.

"Smile, everyone!" Mrs. Moore yelled as Dean and I put our arms around Shannon, who smelled really nice—like peppermint.

"Very nice, guys! Ambrose, can you go and hang with your dad for a few minutes? He needs your help with something."

"Sure, Mom. I'll see you outside, CJ."

After Dean disappeared through the patio door his mom came over to Shannon and me and took a picture of just the two of us. "This is for me." She smiled. "Can you two go and grab the plates and silverware off the counter and take them outside?"

"Sure, Mom."

"Shannon, you smell really nice today."

"You do, too. I almost didn't recognize you with that real shirt on." She smiled and it made the room seem brighter. My heart started beating really fast and it freaked me out.

"Let's go get these outside before your mom kills us."

Dean's birthday was so much fun. His mom really outdid herself. She made monster truck cookies, special monster drinks with his name on the label; I was a little jealous and hoped she could help my mom plan my party in a few weeks. It was just about time to cut the cake and open up the presents.

"All right everyone, gather around the birthday boy so we can get this show on the road. I'm sure your parents are all tired of being here. Or for the lucky ones, they're in no rush to have you home, but I am." The adults laughed at Dean's dad, but the kids huffed and rolled their eyes.

After singing and watching Dean cut into his huge marble cake, decorated with a red monster truck, I helped his mom serve the ice cream and pass it around to everyone. The gate opened before I could sit down and everyone's attention turned to it.

"Sorry, is the party over?"

"No, no it's not, Sally." I ran over to her with an extra piece of cake. "Here take this plate and sit next to the birthday boy, he's over there." I turned and pointed toward the bench in front of the tree.

"Thanks, CJ. I owe you one."

Sally was beautiful, long blonde hair, nice long legs, and she always smelled good, too. Dean was a lucky guy if she agreed to kiss him. If she became his girlfriend that would rock.

"Dude, we did it!"

"What?"

"Kissed."

"Where?"

"Inside the tree house."

"Awesome. Did she agree to be your girlfriend?"

"She said to wait a few days and she'll let me know, but she admitted that she liked me and I told her I really liked her too."

"I don't care how much y'all like each other, you better not ditch me, bro. And I'll let it slide this time, but no more girls in our tree house!"

"I won't. You know me better than that, CJ. Besides, I'm sure you'll have a girlfriend soon and you'll probably ditch me. My bad about the tree house, but that was the only place we could be alone for a few minutes." He elbowed me in the side as I climbed the steps and hopped onto the second bunk.

One day I'll have a girlfriend, and her name will be Shannon Moore.

Chapter 3

My idiot brother started summer school today and it made me really sad. I figured because he'd be gone, CJ wouldn't come over to play with me anymore. Or if he did come over, he'd be bored because I was too chicken to do all of the crazy boy things he and my brother did.

As I pouted on my Rainbow Pony sheets, I wished CJ could come over.

"Knock, knock. Can I come in?"

"CJ?" *That was fast. Good job, magic genie, with the wishes!*

"Yeah, I figured you'd want to go for a walk with me or something. It's really nice out today."

I thought my heart was gonna explode out of my chest. "I—uh—yeah. Did you ask my mom?"

"She gave me the okay, as long as we didn't do anything stupid, like climb trees." He laughed and his voice cracked. "Dangit, it won't stop doing that."

"Whoa, your voice is trying to get really deep. I kind of like it."

"Yeah, well, maybe it'll be nice if I didn't still sound like a squeak toy in between." He laughed.

"Where did you want to go?"

"We can go to the park if you want."

"The park sounds fun."

We walked to the huge playground a few blocks from my house. It was practically empty, which was unusual during lunch time.

"Well, I guess we have the whole place to ourselves. Maybe everyone else had summer school too."

"I guess so."

"So are you excited to start the eighth grade?"

"Yeah, are you excited to start fourth?"

"Kind of. I wish I were older so I could go to middle school."

"Why? Why be in a rush to grow up?"

"I dunno, I just wanna be able to do more things. More fun things without getting in the way or getting hurt."

CJ rubbed my shoulder and then grabbed my hand. "You're never in the way. So tell me, what do you want for your birthday? It's next week you know."

"Promise you won't laugh?"

"I won't."

"I'd like a Rainbow Pony doll."

"Why would I laugh? I know how much you love those things. It looks like Rainbow Pony exploded in your room."

I felt so much better that I could tell him what I really wanted; I hadn't even told my mom what I wanted yet. "Thank you for being so nice, CJ. My brother's always being a jerk to me, so I thought that's how all boys were gonna treat me forever."

"Shan, don't think that way. Dean is just being Dean, but all boys won't treat you like that. He's your older brother—he's supposed to give you a hard time. Besides, you know he'd do anything for you and he'll always be there."

"Will you always be there too?"

He stopped and looked at me. I could see he was trying to think of the right thing to say, but I started to feel sad.

"I'm gonna try, Shannon. I'm really gonna try."

"Sweetheart, what do you want to wear for your party tomorrow?" Mom asked.

"I want to wear the blue and white dress with the sparkly flowers."

"Wow, you've never worn that one before."

"I know, but turning ten is special and I want to wear my special dress."

The dress was a present from my grandmother. She had passed away and that was the last thing she was able to buy me before her memory got all bad.

"Okay, sweetheart. Grandma Rose would be so proud to see you in it; she'll be watching you celebrate from heaven."

"I know, Mom."

"Get some sleep, okay? I want you to be well rested for tomorrow," she said, placing a kiss on my forehead. She looked so tired. I wish I could have helped her in the yard, but she wouldn't let me.

I can't wait for the day I can do grown-up things and help out more.

"Wake up, sleepyhead." CJ had snuck in my room the next morning and startled me.

"What are you doing in my room?"

"Your mom told me to come and wake you up for breakfast."

"What did she make?"

"Your favorite."

"Poop face, get out of bed and come eat," Amby grumbled by my door.

I rolled my eyes and tossed the sheets back. I saw a pair of dirty panties on my floor that hadn't made it into my laundry basket and hoped CJ didn't see it. *Oh my gosh!*

I followed the boys down the stairs and could smell the cinnamon in the air. Mom had made her special cinnamon apple waffles. She only made these on my birthday. I could never get sick of them. She made this special apple butter that you could spread on top and we used Aunt Kara's homemade syrup recipe.

"Mom, I think this is the best batch yet!"

"Yeah, Mom, you really outdid yourself this time. Can I have seconds?"

"Hey, slow down, Mr. Pigglesworth, these are my birthday treat!"

CJ laughed and his voice cracked again. I know he hated it, but I really thought it was cute. I couldn't wait to hear what his voice would sound like when it was fully developed.

"All right, you three, go on upstairs and get ready. The bouncy house is outside and I know you guys will want to test it out before everyone else," Dad said.

The boys ran from the table and I stayed behind and finished every last bite of my waffle, because I knew it'd be another year before I could have it again.

I placed our dirty dishes into the sink and as I finally climbed the stairs, I could hear them flipping around in the bouncy house out back. I looked through the window in the hallway and then ran to toss on my play clothes to join them before the party.

I ran out back to meet the guys and they were giving me a hard time—as usual. Amby was blocking the hole so I couldn't crawl through and CJ laughed at first, and then pushed him out the way so I could climb inside. "You guys suck."

"You love us. What would your life be like if you didn't have your two older brothers in it?" I almost felt sick when he said that, because I didn't see CJ as my brother. He was something much more special. Something I didn't quite understand, but something I wanted.

"I don't know what I'd do without either of you." I smiled at CJ and then my brother. Amby gave CJ a weird look, and then karate chopped him in the chest, knocking him to the floor.

"Don't you catch feelings for her! I love you like a bro, but I'll kill you," he joked.

CJ bounced back to his feet and knocked my brother flat on his back. "Have fun trying; I won't go down without a fight."

As I hopped away from the boys, I noticed how big this princess bouncy house really was. It was like a huge inflatable castle. There was an obstacle course in the back of it and a basketball hoop on the inside. The slide had two options, wet and dry, and I knew that would be a ton of fun later when my friends arrived.

"Guys, go and get changed, the party starts in thirty minutes!" Mom yelled. We all ran out of the castle and inside to change. I was so excited that that day was my birthday, but I was even more excited to find out what CJ got me.

Chapter 4

When Shannon came downstairs in her new outfit, I was in shock. She looked so pretty. She'd told me about the dress before, but it didn't seem like a big deal until she put it on. She looked like a true princess. Her mom had braided her hair and given her a special sash that said "It's my birthday" on it and a tiara to go with her outfit.

I knew her brother would kill me if he knew how I felt about his sister, so I kept it inside. It was safer that way.

I was nervous to give her the presents I'd gotten, because I bought her two completely different things. One she asked for, and one she didn't.

We were all outside playing and I watched as all the smaller kids ran around Shannon, telling her how pretty she was and that they loved her dress.

While everyone was distracted, I went inside to take a peek at the cake and presents on the table. I carefully pushed mine to the front of the pile so she'd see them first. As I was on the way back outside, I heard the Moores' house phone ring. I overheard Mrs. Moore talking to someone, promising to not tell someone something, and when I came around the corner, I could tell I scared her because she slammed the phone on the counter and grabbed her chest.

"Oh, Cody, what are you doing inside, love?"

"I just wanted to make sure Shannon saw my presents first."

"That was very sweet of you. Would you mind going back outside and helping Mr. Moore with the grill for me, please?"

"Okay." Shannon's mom was just as beautiful as her. They looked very similar, but her mom didn't have freckles and she did have big boobs. They had the same long legs, smile, and hair, and were both really nice and welcoming to me.

I walked outside and found Shannon's dad grilling with a beer in his hand. "Hey, Mr. M."

"Hey, CJ. How goes it? Want to learn how to cook the perfect burger?"

"Sure."

After Mr. Moore taught me how to grill a few things, it was finally time for Shannon to open her presents and cut the cake. They'd brought everything out back since it was such a nice day. We all surrounded Shannon, and tears slid down her face as she stood, staring at the cake.

"Why are you crying, honey?"

"This cake is the prettiest cake I've ever seen. I love it so much; I don't even want to eat it!"

"We've taken plenty of pictures. There's no way we'll ever let you forget about this cake, okay, princess?"

"Okay, Daddy."

After a few uncoordinated versions of the birthday song, we all were served cake and ice cream, while Shannon was gawking at her presents on the table. "Do you know which one you want to open first?" I asked, as I stabbed the last piece of cake with my fork.

"This one, with the sparkly paper. I can tell it's from someone special." She looked over at me and smiled.

"Guess you'll have to open it and find out."

She pulled the huge box toward her and her eyes lit up as she shredded the paper off. "Oh my God! Oh my God! Rainbow Pony! CJ, how could you afford this?"

"Don't worry about that. Do you like it?"

"Like it? I love it!" She gave me the biggest hug, and I could feel Dean's eyes burning through my skin.

"What are you trying to do, CJ? Be her boyfriend or something? You got her a better gift than me and I'm her older brother!"

"Maybe if you listened to what she liked and wanted, you would have gotten her something nicer. But, I'm sure she'll like whatever you got her, man."

I'd seen Dean mad before, but this time, he'd been so mad that his cheeks had turned red.

"Okay, open the other gifts, honey. I'm sure you'll love them all!" Mrs. Moore said, trying to change the mood.

After watching Shannon carefully rip the paper off of every other present, she finally finished. She had so much stuff that we all had to make a ton of trips just to clear the back yard. She only kept two presents out: one was the pony I gave her, and the Baby Terry doll her brother had gotten her.

All of her friends left, and just her family and I were sitting outside. "Andrew and Ambrose, would you mind helping me clean up the trash and take care of the kitchen?"

"Sure, but why doesn't CJ have to help?"

His mom sighed, exasperated. "Just come with me, boy!"

I think Mrs. Moore could tell how I felt about Shannon.

"CJ?"

"Yeah."

"I really love the present you got me."

"The Rainbow Pony?"

"I do love that one, but this one is very special." She pulled out the thin silver necklace, which was the second gift I'd gotten for her, with a green amulet hanging from the center. "Would you mind putting this on?"

She handed me the necklace, and I snapped the hooks together behind her neck as she held her hair up. She let her hair down and rubbed the amulet between her fingers.

"CJ, no one has ever made me as happy as you have today. Thank you so much. I hope you stay in my family forever. I couldn't imagine my life without you and my big brother in it."

I smiled, and gave her a hug. She squeezed tightly and then kissed me on the cheek. "Whoa, what was that for?"

"For being special."

"You're pretty special too, kid. Let's go inside and help them clean up. And happy birthday again, my friend."

She grabbed my hand and held it tight. It was hard to breathe, and I never wanted it to end. But, I was scared her family would say something, so I only let her hold it until we got to the back door, then snatched it away.

"It's okay, CJ. Mom and Dad know I like you."

"Yeah, but Dean doesn't."

"Oh, well. One day I'll be older and it won't matter what he thinks."

"I can't wait for that day."

"Me neither. I'll be able to really learn what true love feels like. CJ, can you promise me something?"

"Sure."

"When we're older, do you think we could be boyfriend and girlfriend?"

"Sure, as long as I don't hate you by then."

"Even if you did, I still think deep down you'd still love me."

"Guess we'll find out."

Chapter 5

Every night since my birthday, I'd gone to sleep with a huge smile on my face. Rainbow Pony was by my side, and no matter how much Mom yelled at me to take it off, I refused to take off the necklace that CJ had gotten me. It was very important to me.

Today was another special day—it was finally CJ's birthday. I was so excited. There was this one vintage Mötley Crüe t-shirt at the mall that he'd told me he wanted, but could never afford. I begged Mom and Dad for extra chores around the house so I could buy it and surprise him. Amby questioned me every day about what I was getting him, but I wouldn't tell him because he'd try to outdo my gift.

"Shan, what did you get him?"

"For the last time, I'm not telling you!"

"Mom! Shan won't tell me what she bought for CJ."

"It's none of your business, Ambrose."

"Told ya so, dodo brain!"

"Shut it, poop face!"

"Ambrose, be nice to your sister."

"But she started it!"

"Ambrose Dean!"

"Fine, Mom."

I stuck my tongue out at him, and ran into my room. I looked out my window and saw a really big truck in front of CJ's house. "Mom!" I screeched.

She burst through the door. "What's wrong, honey?"

"What's that truck doing in front of CJ's house?" Mom looked out the window, and then started rubbing her hands against her jeans. That was one of her nervous signs. "Mom?"

"I rather not talk about it, let's just get through the day, and then we'll discuss it later, okay?"

"Okay, Mom."

When CJ came to our house that day, I could tell something was really wrong. He kept his hands in his pockets, he was quiet, and didn't smile one bit. "CJ, what's going on?"

"I don't want to talk about it, Shan. I just want to enjoy what's left of my birthday. Let's make it the best one ever, okay?"

"Of course. I got you the best gift ever!"

"Awesome, I can't wait to see it. I'm going to go change and then maybe we can hang out before the party."

"Okay, I'll be waiting for you on the patio."

"Sounds good."

I sat on the stone ledge of the deck and swung my legs over. The day was really nice; it wasn't too hot, or too cold. The breeze blew my hair all over the place, but I didn't care. I liked having my hair down around CJ.

"Hey, Shan." I looked behind me and CJ looked much better than he did when he showed up at my house earlier.

"Hey, are you feeling better?"

"Not really, this was supposed to be the best day ever and now it's not."

"What's going on?"

"My parents are—I don't want to talk about it."

"Okay, well, your party starts soon, want to go and bounce around the obstacle course?"

"Sure."

CJ's party was much more fun than mine and Amby's, and his smile came back, which was nice. Mom was such a good party planner; it used to be an old hobby of hers. She and Dad were acting strange and I felt like everyone was keeping something important from me. I don't think Amby knew what was going on either, but he was trying his best to make sure CJ was happy. They played, made water balloons, and hit everyone with them—it was pretty funny when Dad got hit in the back with one.

"Okay, everyone, let's cut this cake before it melts," Dad said.

There had to be a bazillion kids at this party, and it made my heart happy, knowing they were all here to celebrate CJ. For the first time in a long time, CJ's parents showed up at our house.

His mom was very pretty. She had long strawberry-colored hair, tan skin, the same brown eyes as CJ, and she was kind of short. CJ's dad looked just like him, minus the beard and blue eyes. If CJ looked like that when he got older, I could tell he'd break a bunch of hearts.

CJ was surrounded by his parents, mine, and all of his friends as we sang happy birthday so loud and awkward, it was the best. He asked for a rock star-themed party and that's exactly what he got. We had inflatable guitars as favors, it was pretty cool. The cake he got was made of ice cream and the little cookie crumbles looked like the little holes on top of a microphone.

I held onto my gift until the very end. I wanted to see the excitement on his face after he opened everyone else's presents.

"Is this everything?" he said as he looked in my direction, and gave me a pouty face.

"Nope, here." I handed him the box I had hidden behind the tree just before we all sang to him.

He ripped opened the box and I thought his heart was gonna explode. "SHANNON! You—I—what the?"

"Try saying thank you, Cody," his mom said.

He ran over to me and picked me up and twirled me around in front of everyone. "Thank you! I'll wear it forever. I've always wanted this."

"I know, friends always listen." I looked over at Amby and he didn't look mad this time, he actually looked really happy.

"Okay, everyone, we need to clean up, because Cody has to leave with his parents. Thank you all for coming, and we hope you enjoyed celebrating him turning thirteen!" Mom said.

"Shannon, I want you to take this letter. Don't open it until later okay? And don't let anyone else see it, promise?"

"Okay, I promise." I tucked it in my shirt for safekeeping.

Dear Shannon,

I don't know how or why this is happening, but I have to move far, far away. They won't tell me where. My dad is being weird and I think he got into some kind of trouble. I don't know if we'll ever come back to Boston, but I'll try to write once we land somewhere. I wish I could see your silly pigtails and sun kisses longer, but if this is the last time, just know that I love you, Shannon.

I always have, and always will. Don't forget about me and I won't forget about you — ever.

Tell Dean I'll never find another cool dude like him, and I know I haven't seen your gift yet, but I bet it's rockin' and I'll cherish whatever it is forever!

Good-bye, for now.

-CJ

I had to read the letter a couple times, because the tears wouldn't stop falling from my eyes. I knew something was up, but I didn't think he'd be moving away.

I miss you and I love you too, CJ. I'll never forget you—ever.

Chapter 6

Cody

Eleven years later

Returning to my hometown after all this time was weird as hell. All the innocent memories from my childhood flooded my mind as I rode the bus into town. I had no money and no place to go, but I had to flee that hell hole in Canada.

I'd heard that my old buddy Dean was still here and worked part-time as a fitness instructor at Get Tight gym. From his online profile, I saw that he was looking to start a band, and I had hoped all the years I'd learned to play guitar would make me a good fit—if he didn't hate me for leaving.

I saw a flyer at the bus station for tryouts right as I got off the bus, so I knew where I needed to be tonight, but I had to get something to eat.

Tossing my duffel bag over my shoulder, I saw a cute girl eyeing me from the back of the line. I shot her my best panty-dropper smile, and knew she was my ticket to a hot meal, and a hot piece of ass.

"Karli, right? Do you think I could use your shower?"

"You can do and use anything you want, Jamison. That was the best sex I've ever had."

And that's where you fucked up. Never tell a man you just

met from a bus station that he had been the best you'd ever had. Good-bye.

Too bad, she was hot as fuck. Her tits were fake, but her blue eyes were pretty, and her ass reeled me in. Her bathroom was next to her bedroom and I quickly grabbed my stuff and took a long hot shower. It was much needed.

After my shower, I'd stuck my head in her doorway and realized she'd passed out. *You've done it again, Jamison.*

She'd let me borrow fifty bucks and normally I'd feel bad, but since she was just as desperate for ass as I was, I took it as gratitude. I couldn't be rude after thoroughly fucking the girl.

I snuck out the front door and walked to the venue where the band auditions were being held. Coincidently, Karli lived just a few blocks away. I had to pawn my guitar to get a bus ticket, but hopefully someone would let me borrow theirs so I could shred.

I walked into the small bar named Charlemagne's and immediately spotted Dean in the crowd. A young blonde with big tits, a barely-there skirt and an okay body greeted me as soon as I came through the door, and handed me a number. "Let me guess, you play the guitar or sing?"

"Both, actually."

"Oh, well, good luck. If you need anything, I'm Samantha, but my friends call me Sam."

"Jamison here. You wouldn't happen to have a spare guitar handy, would you?"

"I'll find you one, give me a few minutes and I'll be back."

"Thanks a lot."

My stomach was in knots as I looked around this small butt ugly place. I didn't know if I should wait until the tryouts were over to say something to Dean, or grow a pair and do it now. I decided on the latter, and grabbed a whiskey on the rocks at the bar to calm the hell down.

A soft tap on my shoulder broke my trance and Sam was behind me with a vintage Gibson guitar in her hand. "This looks almost like the one I had back home."

"Well, it's yours for the audition. If anyone gives you shit, tell them Sam gave it to you."

"I will."

"This is for later, so you can repay me." She slid a piece of paper with her number in my back pocket and brushed her thick lips against my neck. If I hadn't had to prove my worth on that stage, she'd be earning her repayment on her back right now.

The auditions started and the first few were terrible hacks. Most were pimply kids from garage bands, trying to branch out from their moms' basements. I had a couple more shots of whiskey before it was my turn—one to settle my nerves, and two to drown out the shitty people that went on before me.

"Hey, you!"

"Yeah?"

"What's your name?"

"Jamison."

"It's your turn." I walked onto the stage and the look he was giving me seemed like he was ready to punch my face in. "I see you have a familiar looking guitar there, wonder where that came from—*Sam*."

"Shut it, Ambrose, he'll rock the shit out of it—watch."

Oh, so he strictly went by Ambrose now. Calling him Dean would probably freak him the hell out. *Anyway, you need to nail this spread or you're fucked, Jamison.*

I tuned the guitar and played a little to get the sound just right. As I finessed the fret with my left hand, and strummed with my right, I thought of an old song I'd written a few years back and decided it was now or never. Go big, or go home.

Flames, burnt my past away
Flames, cleansed my soul of pain
Flames, flicker day and night
Flames, were so wrong, felt right
Flames, took my life from you
Flames, brought the boys in blue

Flames, as they cuffed me tight
Flames, no more need to fight
The day has come
The demons won
The amber specks of darkness
The truth be told, your lies unfolded
Right in front of us all
Right in front of us all

"Dude, those bars were fucking deep. I'd love to hear more, you're in! Hey—you look kind of familiar. I feel like we've met before."

"Maybe, the world is a small place."

"No shit, we'll talk in a bit. The rest of your drinks will be on the house; this will be your new home now, bro."

"Thanks."

I exited the stage and reclaimed my spot back in front of the bar. The bartender gave me two more whiskeys and before I pulled the first glass to my lips, a soft voice grabbed my attention.

"My name's Alexis, but most people call me Red. I can play back-up on any instrument, but I'm auditioning to be one of the lead singers."

"Go for it."

Oooh, oh, oooh, oh
Love is a battle, a battle leaves scars
The one on my heart, is the worst one by far
The chills from your soul, the touch feels so cold
Deep down in my bones there's no saving me
Oooh, oh, oooh, oh
Don't hate me for what we used to be,
The one you loved died inside of me

The feelings of joy, are now null and void
Nothing is what it used to be
Nothing, oh, nothing, can undo the hell from you
I said nothing, oh nothing, will bring me back to you

Her voice commanded the fucking stage. She had an amazing raspy tone that made each note sound airy, but sexy as hell. I think everyone, including the females, got a boner from listening to her sing those few bars.

Red was every guy's dream girl: petite, with killer long legs, nice firm tits that occasionally popped out of her crop top as she sang, and long black hair with red streaks dyed in the front. Canine bite piercings surrounded her full, juicy lips and she wore a short black skirt with ripped stockings and combat boots. She was definitely my kind of woman.

"Red, you made my assistant cry, you're in. I didn't need to hear another fucking note, because I knew as soon as you told me your name, you were in."

She squealed so loud, I thought she'd resurrect the dead. "Go and join Jamison at the bar and get comfortable, we'll chat later."

"Thank you so much!"

She exited the stage and pulled up a barstool beside me. "I loved your song, did you write it yourself?"

"Yeah. It was an old hobby of mine way back."

"Maybe you can write a few things for this new band. I'm sure we'd do your lyrics justice."

"Maybe you can be my new lucky charm, because my luck has been pretty shitty as of late."

"Sorry to hear that, what are you drinking?"

"Whiskey on the rocks."

"Barkeep, two more rounds and keep 'em coming! To lucky charms!"

"To lucky charms!"

She was hot, could sing, and drink? Fuck, my dick was

going to be in constant agony around her.

After a painful eternity of auditions, no one else had joined us at the bar. Red and I had gotten so drunk that we couldn't quit laughing when someone would fuck up on the stage.

"Well this day was long and torturous, but at least we found two future rock legends out of the duds!" Dean said to his panel.

"Red, Jamison, join us over here!"

We joined Dean and a friend at the table. His assistant bailed for the night and I couldn't blame her—she'd suffered through the auditions from the very start.

"So we need to find a drummer and a keyboardist. Do you two know anyone?"

"I don't," I said, shaking my head.

"I have a friend of a friend I could recommend. He used to be heavy into drugs, but he's a kick-ass drummer," Alexis said.

"What's his name?"

"Reggie."

"Oh, shit, I know that dude. He's sick with the sticks. Tell him to get down here tomorrow; he'd be fucking perfect for this band."

"I'll spread the word."

"Welp, hopefully we'll find some more talent tomorrow. I don't know where the fuck all those posers came from, but it felt like my damn ears were going to bleed."

"My ears have been bleeding ever since Red performed." She smacked me on my shoulder and we all got a good laugh out of it.

It was a few minutes to closing time and Red was long gone. I had learned a lot about my former best friend.

"So, Jamison, where are you originally from?"

"I was born in Canada, but I lived here until I turned thirteen."

"Oh yeah? What happened after you turned thirteen?"

"My mom and dad forced me to move back to Canada."

"Fuck, that sucks."

"What's even worse is, we moved on my fucking birthday."

"That's so fucking weird. My best friend disappeared after his party at my house . . ." Dean trailed off, cocking his head to the side and dropping his beer on the table. "Wait a fucking minute!" He leaned over the table and looked me up and down thoroughly. He was so close, I thought he was going to kiss me. "Jamison . . . CJ?"

"Yeah, Dean, it's me."

"Holy fuck! Dude, I thought you died or some shit. I've tried to find you for fucking ages. And no one's called me Dean since then, either."

"I can't even begin to tell you the hell my father put us through. I thought I was gonna have to change my fucking identity or some shit."

"Dude, that fucking sucks. I took it pretty hard when you left like that, but Shannon—she almost didn't make it."

Fuck . . . Shannon. I promised to write her and never did. She must hate the fuck out of me.

"What do you mean?"

"She went over to your place every single day. Mom caught her trying to break in a few times; it was bad. She just couldn't accept that you were gone. She harassed the mailman for weeks, hoping to hear from you, I just—it was sad, bro. I know you didn't do anything wrong, we were kids, but she was only ten so she couldn't understand."

I suddenly had the urge to puke. And it wasn't due to alcohol consumption, it was due to the fact that the girl I loved, hurt. I never wanted to hurt her, and I hope if our paths ever cross again, she doesn't want to kill me. "Damn, I feel like such a dick."

"Don't man. She didn't try to off herself or anything; she was just depressed for a while. I never brought her around any of my other friends, though; none of them were as tight as us, and

I couldn't put her at risk again. I didn't want something else to happen and send her over the edge."

Fuck. "So where is she now?"

"She's living in an off-campus apartment at college."

"Wow, she's in college? At least one of us is doing something productive with our lives."

"Yeah, after high school I was done with school. I had the attention span of a damn squirrel and refused to pay for something I'd eventually drop out of."

"So what do you do now?"

"I'm a personal trainer, and I'm trying to get this band together so I can quit. I'm trying to get out there, bro. I just need some good peeps and I think we'll have it made."

"That's awesome. Well it looks like I showed up at just the right time."

"I guess so. So where are you staying?"

"I—"

"What's wrong, bro?"

"I don't have a place to stay; I just kind of jumped ship."

"Dude, I have a spare bedroom in my apartment. You're more than welcome to stay with me until you get on your feet again."

"Seriously?"

"Seriously. We've got a lot of catching up to do."

"That's cool," I said smiling. I saw Sam standing in the corner by the bathroom. "I'll be back, there's something I have to take care of first."

"I'll be here," he said, ordering another round.

"I was waiting for you to repay me," she said, as I followed her into the large stall. She unbuttoned my pants and pulled out my cock, her eyes widening before I spun her around and pushed her torso down toward the ground.

"I hope you're flexible, now grab your ankles." I pulled out the last condom I had from my back pocket and rolled it over my length. I lifted her skirt and could smell her slightly musty excitement. I gave her bare ass a smack and pierced her folds with the head of my cock, burying myself as deep as I wanted. She wanted to act like a slut, so I was going to treat her like one.

Chapter 7

After the fuckfest Sam and I had the night before, she hadn't shown up that day. So Dean asked Red and me to assist him with the auditions. Thankfully, there weren't as many as the night before. Alexis told us she got the word to her friend Reg, but he hadn't shown up yet, and so far we hadn't found a half-decent drummer yet. I don't know how Dean put up with this the day before, but everyone we'd heard so far was a hot fucking mess.

A young, pretty-boy looking dude with a keyboard showed up, and Dean didn't seem like he was interested. "Before you start, please tell me you at least know what a middle C and a treble clef are?"

The blond smirked and pressed in between two black keys in the middle of the keyboard with his middle finger. "I like him already," Red said.

"Would you like me to sing do re mi?"

"Don't be a smartass, kid; my time has been wasted for two days and I needed to know if you were the real fucking deal."

"Just listen."

The kid cracked his knuckles, did some sort of relaxation technique with his hands, then he started playing the chorus to "Tuesday's Gone," by Lynyrd Skynyrd. Every single one of our mouths dropped open.

"Holy shit! That used to be one of my dad's favorite songs!"

Alexis said, covering her mouth with her shaky hand. She looked like she was fighting back tears.

"I'm impressed. I didn't think a little pretty-boy shit like you could hold a damn note. You're in. Go have a seat at the bar and you'll be taken care of until this shit show is over."

"What's your name?" I asked.

"Colton."

"How old are you, Colt?"

"Twenty-one."

"Rock on, bro. You better be able to bring the heat to those keys when we need you to."

"You got it. Being in a band has been one of my dreams since I was a kid. I promise not to let you down." He put his keyboard under his arm and hopped off the stage, smiling at Alexis as he walked by and took a seat at the bar.

A few more people came in, and as we were getting ready to wrap up, a guy with bloodshot eyes and a buzz cut came sloshing in, waving two sticks in his hands. "I'm here. This shit ain't over yet, is it?"

"You're lucky she put in a good word for you, dick, we almost locked the door," Dean said.

"My bad, Ambrose. You need to live a little. Chill, bro."

"Shut up and play us a song. Are you coherent enough to do so?"

He took his place behind the bass drum and tapped his sticks together. My first impression of this dude was that he probably could play the drums, but he looked so high off his ass that I didn't think he'd be worth our time. Boy, was I wrong.

"Hey, one of y'all plays the guitar, right?"

"Yes," Dean answered. "Alexis, go up there and assist your 'friend.'"

Alexis grabbed the spare guitar on the stage and tuned it. "What are we playing?"

"'Moby Dick' by Led Zeppelin."

I think everyone's jaw hit the floor, but once his sticks hit those toms, it was all over. Alexis kicked ass on the bass guitar, but Reg definitely stole the show. High or not, this dude was badass and he'd definitely make a great addition to the band.

"You're in. Fuck, dude, you and pretty boy came to play today. Where the fuck was y'all last night? I wouldn't have even opened the door for auditions today."

"I just heard about this shit last night, or my ass would have been here! The last band I was in sucked major donkey piss."

Alexis chuckled loudly. "Man, you still can manage to make me laugh, Reg."

"I could still manage to make you do a few other things, if you'd have me."

"Still a pig, still not interested."

"It was worth a shot."

"All right, we've officially got our band. Let's drink a few rounds and celebrate!" Dean addressed the crowd.

It'd gotten late and we were the only ones left with Mitch, the bartender.

"So now that we have the band, where the hell are we going to practice?"

"Y'all can practice at my place, upstairs is small as fuck, but the basement is huge and I have a sound booth in there," Reg offered.

"No shit?"

"No shit, CJ. We can start tomorrow afternoon if y'all want. I'll text you all my address."

We all met up at Reg's house the next day and he was right, it was definitely small as hell, but it was good enough to practice and create magic.

We'd practiced for hours and ended up with a few more songs we seemed to have pulled out of thin air. I'd never gotten along with a group of strangers so fast in my life. It was weird as fuck, but good.

"Hey, guys, I have to cut out a little early. Kandy isn't feeling well tonight."

"All right, Keys, go and tend to your fiancée!" Reg sighed, rolling his eyes. Colt bolted out the door and we all grabbed a few beers out of the cooler and sat down. "So what the fuck are we going to call ourselves?" Reg asked, as we crowded around the small table in his basement.

"I don't know, but you're acting like a fucking spazz right now," Dean barked.

"Spazz . . . what about Spasm? I don't know about you fucks, but I give the ladies multiple spasms a night," I said.

"You're such a pig, Cody, but I do like that name. Our audiences will experience spasms by our lyrics and kick-ass beats."

"Then it's a deal? Spasm?" Dean asked, taking a pull off his beer.

"Yeah, but we better hit up Colton's pretty-boy ass and make sure he likes it. I wouldn't want to hear his or Kandy's mouth."

> **Me:** Hey Keys, we're naming ourselves Spasm. You in or out?
>
> **Colt:** That name is kick-ass.
>
> **Me:** You better have your ass here tomorrow.
>
> **Colt:** I'll be there, douchler.

"Pretty boy approves."

"Well I'm gonna head out and get some sleep; we have to practice all day tomorrow and unlike you assholes, I need my beauty rest," Alexis said, as she grabbed her oversized purse and launched it over her shoulder. She was wearing the tightest fucking shorts and top that day. The shit she wore constantly made my cock ache, but since she proclaimed herself as a lesbian, none of us would ever get a shot with her. Not even on the coldest day in hell.

Chapter 8

We'd been practicing for weeks and finally had our first show at the amateur night that Charlemagne's hosted on Fridays. The house was packed and I was glad I took a few shots before we took the stage. I'd done a few gigs in the past, but nothing ever this serious, and in front of this many people.

Before we got to the stage, a few assholes Dean knew tried to give us shit, but we pushed through and made it to the front without throwing blows. "Let's get ready to kick some ass," Colt said as we walked onto the platform.

"Welcome to the stage, the band members of—" Tom the stage manager turned toward us, muffling the microphone with his hand.

"Spasm!" Alexis shouted.

"Spasm! That name is kick-ass, good luck, guys and girl!"

"How's everyone doing tonight?" Alexis asked the crowd. She was the best hype man a band could ask for. The place was so small that the crowd was damn near on the stage with us. There wasn't much room to move around and it made me a little nervous, but I knew we would rock this shit.

She did a quick intro, and instead of a normal 5–6–7–8, Alexis turned to us and said "Let's fuck shit up!" Reg slapped his sticks together and we went for it. I started off with a spread finger scale to see what kind of crowd we had that night, and scratched on the guitar like it was the last motherfucking performance of my life. The crowd went nuts and Alexis came in with her powerhouse vocals as I switched to A minor, giving the guitar a softer, mellower tone.

> *You've got to feel to get into the fire – into the fire*
>
> *I've lost control, I don't know how, I've lost the way – oh baby*
>
> *I've given it all I got, but you've pissed me off – creating the fire within*
>
> *The thought of sin, the feel of sin, you made me, you gave me*
>
> *Fuck your life, it's time to go, before I spiral out of control*
>
> *You made me, you gave me*
>
> *No reason to stay, you must burn in the flames of the damned*
>
> *Into the fire, get into the fire*

That was what we'd practiced the day before, and we managed to bring down the house. That was an original song written by Alexis, and it gave me the drive to start writing again. I knew with my sick guitar skills and her badass vocal skills, Spasm would be a force to be reckoned with. We were asked to perform two more songs, and we basically pulled them out of our asses.

"We're out of here, Charlemagne's, continue to fucking rock! Spasm has left the building!" she said, placing the microphone back in its stand.

As we exited the stage, Tom and his crew looked at us, damn near speechless. "Ho-how would you guys like to have a regular gig here? You can go on before we host our amateur nights on Fridays. We have our five dollar beers-n-burgers deal and having a house band before the more questionable talent would bring in so much money and fans for you! Plus, it'd help us out a lot, because people tend to start running out of the door once amateur night begins."

"How much would we get paid?" Dean, the responsible one,

asked.

"Five hundred per song, maximum of three songs, I'm not rich."

"I'm fucking in, that's three hundred a piece, non-taxed. I'm so fucking game!"

"Awesome, you guys come and fill the paperwork out tomorrow afternoon and we'll get you on the roster for next Friday." Tom shook all of our hands and paid for a round of beers at the bar for us.

"I can really dig this! First stop bars, next stop fucking Hollywood!" Reg shouted as we all clinked our beers together. "To Spasm, the hottest thing to rise out of a vagina since yeast!"

"You're so fucking gross, dude," Colt said, sputtering on his beer.

"You guys were fucking amazing!" some random girl squealed at us as we sucked down our drinks at the bar.

"Thanks?"

"Would you please sign my boobs? I know you guys will be famous soon and I want to be able to tell people you signed my tits before it happens."

So it's going to be one of those nights.

Dean ran off and started chatting it up with two broads. They were both brunette, and both looked hot. I ran my hands through my hair and jogged to catch up with them.

"Hey, Dean, where are we gonna put this stuff, so we can really celebrate?"

"We can lock it up in the office until we're ready to go."

"Cool, that sounds good. So who do we have here?" I looked both of the ladies up and down and the second brunette gave me a weird look. As he introduced the first girl, Penelope, I believe he said, I couldn't tear my eyes away from the other girl.

"And this is—"

"Shannon," I interrupted, as I gazed at the familiar freckles across her cheeks. Sun kisses, we used to call them. She immediately freaked out and bailed. *Shit, that was not the reaction I was looking for.*

Four out of the five of us shut down Charlemagne's and made a few—well, a lot of fans, in the process. Every single one of us were given free drinks all night. Colt bailed on us because he's pussy-whipped by his fiancée Kandy; she had total control of his balls. But the rest of us stayed. I got a few numbers, couple of blowjobs in the bathroom, you know—the usual life of Cody Jamison before I came back to the States. Being the lead guitarist definitely had its perks and I couldn't wait until we rocked this place every week, giving us all steady income to prove this was more than just some stupid hobby. But no matter how many girls locked their jaws on my cock that night, I couldn't get over seeing Shannon and how much she'd changed. I also couldn't get over the fact that she fucking ran before we got a chance to talk.

"Hey, guys, I'm gonna head out. I'm tired as fuck."

"Me too," Dean chimed in.

"Aww, do you have to go, CJ? I'd like to perform a little show for you." Some random blonde broad meowed in my fucking ear.

"If you didn't just sound like a fucking cat in heat, I would have considered it, but fuck that. See y'all later."

"Fuck you! You don't know what you're missing. You could've had the best night of your life," she spat, running her hands up and down her fake-ass tits.

"Nah, I'm good. My man Reg might be interested though."

Reg's eyebrows pinched together as he slammed his half-empty beer on the table. "Fuck you, Cody!"

I blew him a kiss, tossed my leather vest over my shoulders and jumped off the uncomfortable-ass stool. "Hey, Mitch, if you really want us here every week, can y'all please tell Tom to get some new seating? Christ! I feel like I'm sitting on a hay bale lined with shards of metal."

"You got it, CJ! Only the best for those sweet cheeks."

"Damn straight. Later."

"I'm worried about my sister; she's not answering my calls or texts."

"I'm sure I had a big part in her disappearing act. I feel like major shit that she still hates me."

"She doesn't hate you. I just think she needs time to adjust to that fact that you're back. Hell, I can barely comprehend that you're back after all of this time, bro."

"I know, but do you think she'll be okay?"

"Yeah, we'll go and search a few places before we head back to my place."

"Deal."

Chapter 9

Shannon

"Pen, how does this make me look? You know how much I hate going out," I whined as I tugged at the tight material, pressing against my thighs.

"I'd hit it."

My friend was dragging me out to the bar against my will, but I really needed to get out. I'd been writing and researching for weeks, trying to think of the next big thing to help skyrocket my journalism career. I needed to come up with something that would get me to the top of my class.

"We're going to Charlemagne's tonight, so I hope you're prepared to drink your ass off."

"Why?"

"Because it's amateur night. Local bands will be there, playing live. Plus, your brother will be there, so we'll have lots of protection."

"Ugh, I forgot all about his little band thing. Are they playing tonight? I don't even know who's in the band."

"Who cares? You're going out to get drunk and have a good time—maybe you'll get laid."

"Okay, we'll see. You told me that last time, and I ended up puking on the guy I was dancing with."

"That was a great fucking night—haha."

"Screw you, Pen."

"He still wanted to sleep with you."

"I'm sure he pitied me because I puked on his shoes."

"That's the past. Let's go before you make us late!"

The crowd was pretty live that night. I texted Amby and told him we were coming so we'd get in for free. That was the perk of having a well-known brother.

We took our rightful spots in front of the bar and Pen ordered us drinks. "Here, try this." Penelope smirked as she slid the shot glass full of creamy liquid in front of me.

"What is it?"

"Just try it."

She counted to three and we licked the sugar off the rim, then both tipped our cups back, letting the sweet-smelling liquid slide down our throats. "That was delicious, what was it?"

"Birthday cake shot."

"I've never had one of those before, I want another."

She motioned for the bartender to bring another round of shots. An emo grunge band was playing on stage. Their music wasn't really my type, but most of the crowd seemed to enjoy it. The lead singer looked like that guy from the movie *The Crow*—long dark hair, pale skin, and heavy, dark circles around his eyes. The others looked semi-normal, but they were all dressed in black.

As they exited the stage, another band came through the door and they seemed to get into it. I couldn't see who they were, and turned back to Pen as she placed another shot in front of me. Penelope had been my best friend since we were kids. She knew everything about me, and I knew everything about her. Sometimes I hated going out with her because she was a scumbag magnet. It sucked, because she was gorgeous. Long auburn hair, perfect breasts, a nice ass, long tanned legs, and she wore very subtle makeup. The piercing over her lip gave her look a little edge and I envied that she could put on anything and look great. I had to wear my extra-padded push-up bra to give the illusion I actually had a decent rack, and I was more muscle than curves, sprinkled with freckles. I took up track as a kid to help me get over CJ's disappearance, and still run regularly for stress relief and exercise.

I quickly threw back the second shot and asked for another as the new band was setting up. A petite female with long, dark hair emerged from the group of four guys and took her place at the microphone after their band name was announced. I realized my brother was up there, tuning his guitar, and there was another guy warming up on a guitar that looked awfully familiar.

I carefully watched him tune his guitar, trying to figure out who he was. He wore a leather vest, his tight white t-shirt perfectly molded to his body. His biceps were tightening and releasing as he got himself situated. His denim jeans hugged him in all the right places and I swore I could see the outline of his cock through them. His chestnut hair was disheveled and the few days of stubble that lined his jaw was just pure perfection. My nipples hardened in response to watching him, pressing against the thin black dress I was wearing.

"How's everyone doing tonight?" The crowd erupted with cheers.

"I'm Red, and these assholes are Ambrose, Reg, Colt, and CJ. Hope you're all ready to be thoroughly seduced by the music of Spasm." She turned and whispered something to the group and then they began to play their first song.

CJ? I left my seat and tried to get a closer look. *That can't be my CJ, could it? No, he hasn't been seen in over eleven years. Relax Shannon, go back to your seat.* I returned to our spot and slumped down in my chair.

"What was that all about? You look like you've just seen a damn ghost."

"I think I have." I motioned for another round because I knew I wouldn't be able to keep my composure if I wasn't drunk.

They played a brand new song that I hadn't heard before and I was a little bummed because my brother usually called me and asked me for my feedback on his music before he played live. He knew I was always honest with him when it came to his music, but I guess he was so excited about being in this band, that he didn't think to call me. They all seemed to be talented, and I envied that he already had his dream and career going, while I was trying to get mine in order.

Oh, yeah yeah – my love is gone
Hey, yeah yeah – can't focus on anyone
What you wish for, I cannot achieve
So please stay away from me
I'm begging you, stay away from me
I'm incomplete, I'm broken
Only pain I will bring
The torture inside makes it hard to
Breathe
Breathe
Breathe
I won't stop, I can't stop, get out of my life
Stay away I'm no good, there's demons inside
Everything is different now, I've thrown it away
My future is clear, far from you, I must steer
Breathe
Breathe
Breathe,
The air in my lungs is suffocating me
I lie in wait, as the tables turn; my soul is damned for eternal burn
Stay away from me
Please stay away from me

After the first two songs, they were asked to play an encore, and since they were the last band of the night, the owners allowed it. This time they played a song titled, "Burn It To the Ground."

Burn it to the ground

I wish I could be stronger, but my wishes never come true

Sometimes I wish I could feel, but that's not easy to do

The evil is deep, my insides bleed

I will not feed your fucking monster anymore

Twist and turn, I'll let it burn, the knife that sears through

My skin I yearn

Deeper and deeper the metal becomes a part of me

Deeper and deeper the ash surrounds the

Burn it to the ground

Burn it to the ground

Burn it to the ground

The windows smashed, the metal clashes, I hear your screams, but I'm not rational

The fear inside makes me unemotional

The amber flames of hell, flicker against the hood of my car

The cherry paint's illuminated so well

Burn it all straight to hell. Burn it all straight to hell

Burn it to the ground, I've burned it to the mother fucking ground

The crowd erupted in loud cheers and whistles. Pen grabbed my arm and yanked me toward the stage. "You gonna go and talk to the guy you've been eye fucking since he walked on the stage?"

"No, I think it's him, Pen. I don't think I can do this."

"Him, who?"

"Cody."

"No way! That's Cody? Fuck, he's beautiful."

"I think so? He looks a little different, but those eyes, those chocolate brown eyes, are still the same."

"Shit, what are you gonna do?"

"Leave."

"Aw c'mon, Shan, you can't leave, you need to go and talk to him. Find out why the fuck he never wrote after he promised. He had to have come back for a reason; maybe it was you."

"But why after all these years would he come back just for me?"

"Maybe he was scared. Or maybe he was held by the mob wherever he was and couldn't escape until now." She laughed.

I reached back for my last shot and inhaled it. Ambrose ran over to us before I had a chance to compose myself. I tried to give myself a pep talk. *You can do this.*

"Hiya, Ambrose." It made me so sick the way she flirted with my older brother.

"Penelope. Wow, look who resurfaced from her sea of books."

"Ha-ha," I sassed.

"You guys enjoy the show?"

"You guys fucking rock! Y'all will get picked up by a scout for sure!" Pen said.

"I hope so. I've never felt so sure of something in my life."

"Hey, Dean, where are we gonna put this stuff, so we can celebrate?"

Dean. *No one has called him that in years.*

"We can lock it up in the office until we're ready to go."

"Cool, that sounds good. So who do we have here?" He looked us both up and down, and as my brother introduced Penelope, I couldn't tear my eyes away.

"And this is—"

"Shannon," he interrupted. As his eyes bore into mine, an intense fire erupted inside of me, and all I could think to do was run away.

"Shan? Where are you going?"

Far away from here.

I'd hailed a cab and directed the driver to drop me off at the library. Say what you want, but this was my sanctuary when I needed to think. They were closed, so I sat on the front steps with my head resting in my hands, trying to fight back the ugly cry that was floating to the surface.

I was so young when CJ left, but all the things I felt came right back when he laid his eyes on me. I always thought he'd look as handsome as his dad when he was older, but he proved me wrong—he was even better looking than his father.

When I had agreed to go out that night, CJ was the last person I expected to see, but now that I know he's back in town, I don't know if I can handle it. *What if we reconnect and he hates the person I've become? What if I hate the person he's become? What if we can't get along at all?*

As I sat on the steps, lost down memory lane, my phone rang and buzzed in my purse, snapping me out of it.

> **Pen:** Dude, please tell me you're still alive?
>
> **Me:** Yeah, I just needed to get away and think.
>
> **Pen:** Okay, don't scare me like that ever again! Please let me know when you get home.
>
> **Me:** I will.

Chapter 10

That was not the happy reunion I'd been hoping for. It hurt like hell that I still affected her like that all these years later. I wasn't expecting to see her that night, but damn, she was just as beautiful as ever. Her brown hair was in curls down her back, her brown eyes looked lighter, and her body—damn, she had a nice runner's body. Thick thighs, long legs, nice round ass, and her tits—wow. She definitely wasn't that ten-year-old girl I remembered.

I felt like shit that she ran off like that. We'd spent the better half of that night trying to find her. Dean and I went back to his place, because we figured she just didn't want to be seen, especially by me. Around three in the morning, Dean got a text from her saying she was fine, which was a huge relief.

"Dude, I did not expect her to react like that."

"I don't even know what to say about that. She'll come around, and maybe then you can talk to her. But, for now give her some space, all right, bro?"

"All right."

"So, what exactly happened to you? Why did you have to move away like that?"

"I need a few more drinks before I can open that can of worms. I'll tell you in due time, I promise."

"I can respect that. Let's get some sleep because we need to rehearse later for tomorrow's show."

I awoke to the sun shining directly in my face through the cracked blinds. *Fuck.*

My phone was buzzing like crazy on the coffee table.

"Sup, Dean?"

"Dude, it's your turn to bring the coffee and bagels from Smallie's Bakery."

"Seriously? Fuck, I barely even know where to go or what to get."

"You'll figure it out, asshole. It's around the corner from Reg's place and Keys' mom has our order already."

"I'll make sure to get you a cream puff pastry with extra bitch inside, just how you like it."

"Wouldn't have it any other way, asshole."

"See you in an hour."

After a quick shower and a fresh change of clothes, I walked to the bakery and grabbed the band's favorite coffees and pastries. Colton's dad owned the joint, so we got the deep family discount—free.

I made my way around the corner to Reg's shack. It wasn't really a shack, but it was a cramped two-bedroom in the middle of the ghetto that shouldn't have even counted as a two-bedroom because the second bedroom was basically a glorified closet. The basement did make up for the lack of space upstairs. There were a few ragged leather couches and a table in front of the studio, and that's where Spasm created all of our magic.

I placed the bags and trays down on the table. "Here, come and get your shit so we can practice and prepare for tonight."

We'd practiced all damn day and were nice and ready for the performances we had. The first stop was at some dingy bar on the south side of town. We'd never been there before and swore after that night that we'd never go there again. The place was fucking disgusting. The stools there made the stools at Charlemagne's feel like soft, cushiony pillows.

There were planks missing from the wooden bar, and the stage looked so rickety I didn't want to chance performing on it, so we performed on the floor in front of it. We got paid and quickly left. None of us were feeling it, and only half-assed the performance.

"Who the fuck got us that gig? I never want to go through that again," Reg bitched.

"Listen, we're still unknown, so it's all I could fucking get, all right?" Dean barked. "We got fucking paid and that's all that matters. The next spot will be a gem, I promise."

We hopped on the train to the next town over, and as soon as we arrived at Stallion's, a bar with a big neon horse on the top of the illuminated words, I knew we'd hit the fucking jackpot.

Once we walked through the huge, weighted doors, we could hear a band already performing and they sounded awesome. But once we saw who it was—we all cracked our knuckles. It was our rival band, Spearmint Patty. Yes I know, fucking corny as shit, but despite the bad blood between us, they were good. It's just that we were way fucking better.

As they exited the stage, they came toward us. "Well, well, well, if it isn't Spazz ass."

"Fuck you, Jude. Why don't you go touch up your eyeliner, you fucking dick." I shoved my way past him and his emo-ass band, to get to the huge stage. We all tuned our instruments, made sure the amps were plugged in, and made sure the microphones worked. Reg had been sabotaged plenty of times by bands that performed before him, and that shit wasn't going down that night.

"How's everyone doing tonight?" Alexis asked. A few perverts in the front row were whistling and gawking at her so hard I thought their tongues and dicks would hit the floor. She gripped the mic with her gloved hands and belted out a loud note, Reg tapped his drums, Colt hit his keys, and Dean and I strummed our guitars.

Chapter 11

Shannon

I'd dragged myself into my apartment at some ungodly hour in the morning. Pen somehow figured out where I was and made me hang out with her to try and get over CJ's surprise return. I texted my brother to let him know I was okay, because I knew he was probably out looking for me. I didn't want to run into either of them.

My head hurt so bad that I swallowed what felt like half a bottle of aspirin and crashed on the couch.

Bang! Bang! I heard someone pounding at the front door. My head swam with the sudden vertical movement as I jerked upright on the couch.

"What the hell? Who is it?"

"Open the door, bitch. I know you're still in the clothes from the night before and are probably hungry as hell. I have Cappy's with me." I jumped off the couch and stumbled over the coffee table, trying to get to the door. "See, you need me right now."

"Shut up," I grumbled as I unlocked the door.

"Whoa, you look like shit."

"Well, hanging out all night with your ass didn't help. Besides I was so exhausted I crashed on the couch."

"You poor thing. Sit down and eat, then please go shower." She pinched her nose with her free hand and shook her head at me.

"Shut up, I'll shower first and you better have the wine chilled by the time I get back."

"Sir, yes, sir!"

I walked down my narrow hallway, leaving Pen in the living room, and headed straight for the bathroom. I rubbed my temples as I took a long gander at myself. *I look like complete hell.* The bags under my eyes aged me and the smeared mascara and lipstick made me look like a hooker who'd been out all night on a binge run and hadn't cleaned herself up. *Gross.* Somehow my hair had managed to retain its bounce. I reached over the tub and turned the dial to the hottest temperature I could stand, gathered my hair into a messy bun on the top of my head and slid my clothes to the floor.

As I stepped inside the mini-sauna, two thoughts went through my mind: the thought of seeing CJ, and the thought of seeing him naked between my legs.

What is wrong with me? I shouldn't be thinking like this, but I couldn't help it. As the water soothed my sore shoulders, I slid my hands up and down my body, lightly massaging myself as thoughts of naked CJ shuffled through my mind. *Maybe talking to him again wouldn't be a bad thing.* I rubbed myself to relieve the pressure that was building and almost doubled over from my orgasm.

"Quit fingering yourself in there and get out here before your chicken is as cold as your wine!" Pen yelled, snapping me back to the reality that something may truly be wrong with me.

I jumped out and toweled myself off, before I tossed on a tank and some boy shorts and returned to the couch. Pen plopped a plate full of chicken, rice and beans on my lap and I shoveled everything into my mouth, barely breathing as I devoured the delicious meal. "Christ, when's the last time you've eaten?"

"I don't remember, two days ago?" I mumbled, as I shoveled more food into my mouth.

"Okay, we've been friends for eons and I've never seen you eat like this. What the fuck is going on, Shan?"

Ugh, what isn't going on? "Listen, I'm not in a good place right now. I'm overly stressed about my school assignment, and I don't know what to think about CJ's return. I'm just—ugh!"

"Why don't you quit being a pussy and just talk to the man? I could feel the sexual chemistry between you two the moment you realized it was him. Yes, it's been eleven years, but this could be a good thing. Don't think; don't let your feelings get in the way. Just—let how you feel rise to the surface and be upfront and honest with him. *Hey, CJ, I missed you, wanna bang?* See, easy!" We both laughed so hard that I almost choked on my chicken.

"Thanks, Pen. I can always count on you to get my head out of my own ass."

"Duh, that's what besties are for, bitch! Now, let's crack open the bubbly and strategize!"

Pen and I had gotten so drunk that at some point in time I'd invited my brother and CJ over to my apartment.

"Oh my God! What have I done? What did you let me do?"

"That was all you, but I suggest you put something else on to cover those sweet cheeks of yours, unless you want to give it up to CJ tonight. I wouldn't be upset at all. I could distract Ambrose."

"Gross."

"I didn't mean I'd fuck the guy. Geez. I meant I'd make him take me out for a walk or some shit."

"Oh, yeah. That would be a great idea!"

As I chugged back the last bit of wine, my doorbell rang. "They're here!"

"Go and toss something on, I'll keep them in here."

As she went for the door, I booked it down the hall into my room, slamming the door behind me. My mind was cloudy and I couldn't think straight. *Should I wear a dress? Pants? A skirt? What the hell was I thinking? Yoga pants for the win!*

I could hear CJ talking to Pen, and the deep, richness of his voice almost calmed me. It had this weird soothing effect on me, just like it did when we were younger. Cracking open the door, I could only see the back of his head, but the smile that appeared on Pen's face told me everything I needed to know. She'd forgiven him for me.

He turned around and those eyes pierced my soul, completely obliterating all those feelings of loss, sorrow and despair. My knees felt weak and the sound of my heartbeat roared in my ears as I tried to force a smile on my face.

"Hey, Shan."

"Hey, CJ."

"Do you think we could go somewhere a little more private and talk?"

Pen interrupted, not giving me the chance to open my mouth. "Listen, I know you guys had some kind of weird underage love affair—sorry Ambrose—but maybe we could all just hang out, get a feel for each other, and then you guys can hang out, before things get weird."

"Okay, I can respect that, but only if that's what Shannon wants." His eyes searched mine and my brain turned to mush.

What is it that Shannon wants, exactly?

"We can talk. I think eleven years is long enough not to talk. Pen, I'll be okay. Follow me, CJ."

I led him through my room and opened the window beside my bed. I climbed out first, and then waved him on to follow me onto the fire escape. The sounds of our footsteps echoed on the metal flooring as I found a step to sit on. He remained standing. The cool breeze blew against my warm skin, briefly cooling me off, until CJ placed his hand on my shoulder. "I'm sorry, Shannon. I have waited eleven fucking years to tell you that face-to-face."

"I don't know if I can accept that. I mean, you just up and left . . . no letters like you promised, no call, nothing. It was like you ceased to exist. I couldn't get over you; hell, even now I can't get over you. No guy that I ever talked to could live up to the hype I built up about you. No guy was ever good enough."

He stepped back, running his fingers through his hair in

front of me. His jeans clung to his legs, and his white t-shirt complimented his muscular torso. "Shan, no girl was ever good enough for me, either. I could never replace what I felt for you. I know we were just kids, but that was more than puppy love. In my eyes, it was something much deeper, something that went straight to my core and branded my heart."

I could feel myself trying to choke back the tears. I couldn't believe how deep of a connection he'd felt for me. I was so dumb and naïve, but I still couldn't get over the fact that he left, ruining everything I'd planned in my head. It was all mapped out in my crazy ten-year-old brain: the kids we'd have, the house we'd buy.

"CJ, I—"

He leaned in and silenced me with a kiss. His soft lips melted against mine, wrapping me up like smooth silk and devouring the resistance I once had. It was like our lips were made for each other.

"I'm sorry, but I had to do that. I had to know what your lips tasted like." With our noses mere inches from each other, I grabbed the back of his neck and went in for more.

"And I need to be sure this will be worth the trouble."

"It can be."

"I know it's too soon, but I want you to know that I'm not looking for anything serious."

"Shannon, it wouldn't be right if we tried to jump back in where we left off. We're like two distant strangers. We'll play it by ear and see how it goes."

"Deal."

CJ and I were on the fire escape talking for what felt like forever. Amby and Pen came to check on us several times, making sure we hadn't pushed one another over the edge yet, but we were fine. We chose not to bring up the past, because it would be like ripping off a bandage that'd been on for a few days, stuck on your arm hair. You know it's gonna hurt like hell when you rip it off, and neither of us were drunk enough to handle that.

He'd told me about his passion with music and that being back in this city and back around us inspired him to write. He'd even given me a sneak peek of a song he'd been working on called "Missing Pieces."

"All right, love birds, we need to head out, and apparently get lots of coffee, because we need to go right to practice in an hour," Ambrose grumbled from the window.

"Okay. Shannon, make sure you come to the show tonight, okay?"

"Oh we will, Mr. Jamison!" Pen sassed.

We both climbed back through the window, one by one, and Pen had the cheesiest smile on her face. "What?"

"So was he the one that got away?"

"I'm not sure."

"Well, by the bright red glow of your cheeks, I'd say there's a huge possibility."

"Whatever, go fix me breakfast. We need to go shopping; I need to look good tonight."

"And why is that?"

"I think I may do something a little unorthodox for Shannon Moore."

"And what might that be?"

"Sleep with a ghost I used to be in love with."

"Ghost?"

"Well, he's alive, but the love I felt was for someone I knew eleven years ago."

"I'll never understand your logic at all."

"You're not supposed to." I winked.

I'd decided to take another break from studying that night and Pen threatened to cut me if I pulled a pen out or even attempted to work on my assignment. I don't normally go out this much, but seeing CJ again made me feel a little reckless.

The band was performing at a bar called The White Horse and it was another packed house. As Pen and I took our seats in front of the bar, we had a full view of the stage. It was nice and sturdy looking, unlike the one at Charlemagne's. That place was due for some serious remodeling.

The line-up was posted on the side of the stage on an electric screen and Spasm was on first. Pen slid some weird concoction in front of me and I chugged it down without even thinking. "That was delicious, get me a few more."

"Someone's rambunctious tonight."

"I can't explain it, Pen, I feel different."

"You'll feel even better once Cody Jamison buries his cock deep inside of you."

I elbowed her in the side and she cackled loudly. The host announced Spasm and the crowd went nuts. "Looks like they're gaining popularity."

"All the more reason you need to fuck him now, so you can claim him before they blow up."

"How's everyone doing tonight?" The host addressed the crowd. A few people cheered, but once he mentioned Spasm was the first performance of the night, the whole place came to life.

Alexis took her rightful place in the center of the stage, grabbing the microphone with her gloved hand.

"How are you sexy mother fuckers doing tonight?" The crowd stomped their feet and cheered and whistled for Alexis. "Good, now listen up. We've got a brand new song written by our own Cody Jamison, so you better listen the fuck up! Oh and ladies, he's single, so try not to attack him all at once."

That hurt to hear. Technically he was single and free to do whatever he wanted, but the pang in my chest told me otherwise. I wanted him and I don't think I could handle hearing or seeing him with someone else.

Missing . . . pieces
Missing . . . pieces

Dum de da
Dum de de da
I'm empty
A lost girl
Dum de da
Dum de de da
The only one from this world
A puzzle, not finished
Unquenchable disturbance
A whole space of shadows
Embrace me as I follow
Dum de da
Dum de de da
I'm empty
A lost boy
Dum de da
Dum de de da
The only one from this world
I'm incomplete
Untouchable feat
Running free and discouraged
Dum de da
Dum de de da
We're empty
We're lost ones
Dum de da
Dum de de da
We've found each other in this world

The sample he'd given me on the fire escape was nothing compared to hearing the live rendition of it. My entire body was covered in goose bumps and it felt like that song had a special meaning. I felt like that song was written just for me.

"Shan, are you all right?" Pen looked at me like she was concerned for my wellbeing.

"I'm fine, why?"

"Because your jaw has been on the floor since the song started."

"He gave me a little sample of it last night and it was just surreal hearing it live."

"Oh, now I get it. Let's go!"

"Where are we going?"

"You need to go and talk to him."

"Geez, Pen, they just finished unhooking their instruments."

"And? Oh the drummer is hot as fuck, maybe he'll talk to me this time."

Penelope had it bad for Reg, but he wouldn't give her the time of day. He would never tell her why; he'd just say a few words to her and then continue ignoring her. It pissed me off quite frankly; she deserved a little more respect than that.

We were right in front of the stairs and my brother Ambrose noticed us immediately. Once he saw what I was wearing, he looked me up and down and shook his head with disapproval, but I was a grown woman and I didn't care what he thought.

"What are you guys doing here? Stalking us?" Colton smiled, gripping his keyboard under his muscular arms. He was going to be off the market soon, but he was hot too. Short blond hair, clean shaven, bright blue eyes, nice tight athletic body with a few tattoos . . . He was definitely the hot boy next door.

I pointed at Penelope. "She dragged me out—again."

"Good, you need to lighten up," he said.

"I know." CJ walked down the stairs next and my heart pounded against my chest. My breath ran short, and my legs felt like they were going to slip from underneath me when he flashed me his killer white smile. His chocolate brown eyes bore into mine and I felt like I was going to dissolve into a puddle in the middle of the floor.

"Hey, Shannon. Glad to see you again."

"Yeah, well, we said we'd be here."

"Thank you for coming. Let me put this away and I'll buy you a drink."

"Wait, didn't you guys take the train in?"

"Yeah, but Kandy's outside with the van. The damn thing is finally fixed. It's a piece of shit, but we can't afford to get anything else. You know, life of a wannabe rock star."

"You guys will definitely have your time to shine, don't you worry. You guys are so talented and you're so ho—" *Shut up, Shannon.*

"So what?"

"Nothing. Go put your stuff up and I'll be at the bar waiting for you."

He disappeared into the crowd, not without a few interruptions by groupies in skirts so tight, I thought they'd split if they sneezed or coughed. The rest of the band walked out the door and Pen and I made our way back to the bar. Another band was setting up and I couldn't wait to get drunk and rock out.

Pen and I were sitting at the bar awaiting the band's return when a bunch of drunk college jocks approached us. They were slurring their words and flexing their muscles, trying to get our attention. "Are you guys fucking kidding me? Get out of here," Pen snapped. Waving her hand in dismissal.

"Come on, baby. I'll make your knees weak and fuck you so good, you'll be begging me for more." *Ugh what a pig.* Two of the guys looked like twins—they both had red hair, with freckles, and dark eyes—eyes full of lust. They got so close that I thought I'd get a buzz from the smell of alcohol on their breath. I wanted no part of it, and I must have been giving off some kind of homing signal, because suddenly the guys were pulled away from us. I turned around and Ambrose and Reg were ready to fight, while CJ was pushing his way through the crowd to back up his boys.

"That's enough," said the huge guys with the words security emblazoned across their shirts. "Don't make us kick your drunk asses out. Are you ladies all right?"

"Yes," we agreed and nodded together.

The drunks left with some muttered grumbling and the bandmates came and joined us at the bar. CJ sat right beside me and I instantly felt a chill go down my spine. The hairs on my arms were standing straight up and little bumps were forming on my skin. *Crap, I hate that he has that kind of effect on me.*

"So." His voice was deep and mellow. "What can I get for you, Shan?"

"I'll have a Nutty Irishwoman."

"What the hell is that?"

"Just order the drink. According to Pen, I've been drinking Frangelico and I don't want to mix my liquor. I'm a lightweight."

He ordered the drink and the bartender—a very attractive female one at that—smiled and quickly tossed the Irish cream and hazelnut liqueurs in a shaker. She put it in a nice martini glass and garnished it with cookie crumbs, slid it over, then grabbed the Jack and Coke he asked for.

"How much?"

"This round is on the house," she said with a seductive smile.

Ugh, typical. I rolled my eyes, glad I already had my drink in hand, because I'm sure she'd spit in it after the death glare I'd just given her.

One sip of the creamy drink and I was in heaven. The cookie crumbs accented it just perfectly and I knew I'd want another, but not from her.

"So, Shan, how've you been? How's school treating you?"

"Good, I'm trying to think of something to get me to the top of my class. I need to cook up something big, if I expect to get a real journalism job."

"I'm sure you'll think of something good."

He flashed his signature Jamison smile and I felt my panties dampen in between my legs. I wish I could act on these impulses, but thoughts of my brother's reaction gave me pause.

Before I could finish the drink, another one was on its way over, made by another bartender, thank goodness. A few bands had come and gone, and then a DJ by the name of Snake set up. After his equipment was ready, the feel of the place changed. It felt more like a nightclub.

I hadn't realized how huge the dance floor was until the crowd had separated. The lights dimmed, and the fog machines and strobe lights started swirling around the room. He put on my favorite song by Pitbull, "Culo." I don't know what it was about that fast-paced song with the Spanglish lyrics, but I lost it every time I heard it on the dance floor.

Penelope grabbed my arm and yanked me onto the dance floor. She knew I couldn't resist this song when it came on, plus I'd already had a few drinks in me.

Pitbull was rapping and as the chorus dropped, everyone yelled "Culo" at the same time. Pen and I were grinding against each other without a care in the world. Then in some weird turn of events, Reg came over and cut in between Pen and me, while a pair of arms wrapped around my hips from behind. I looked over my shoulder to see CJ smiling and bent over to show him what I could really do with my hips. He gladly accepted it and gave it right back to me. Everything felt natural with him.

You know that feeling you get when you're having a good time, but something feels *off*? Well, that *off* feeling was my brother, Ambrose. He was lurking at the edge of the crowd, staring at me, and I hated when he looked at me like that. Time to move on.

"I have to pee."

"I'll come with; don't need those assholes bothering you again," said CJ.

As we navigated through the crowd together, and down the narrow hallway, I went inside the ladies' room and he stood guard in the hallway.

After I went to the bathroom and freshened up, I splashed a little cold water on my face, and then added a fresh spritz of perfume. I always wore waterproof makeup when I went out; if not, I'd look like a damn raccoon by now.

I walked out of the bathroom and CJ was facing the opposite direction, so I was greeted with a nice view of his tight ass in his jeans. "I'm good now."

He turned around and smiled at me. He looked over his shoulder and then stalked toward me, which was weird because the dance floor was the opposite direction. Honestly, I was sure he'd be surrounded by a crap ton of groupies by now.

Something was different. I don't know if it was the way he walked, or the way he was looking at me, but it was almost like he was silently staking his claim on me. We agreed to take things slow, so I was confused.

He backed me into the wall, with his hands resting on either side of my head. His brown eyes, darkened with lust, made me hot all over. I could feel my cheeks flush at the thought of being with CJ. His eyes connected with mine, and he lightly ran his fingers down my cheeks and down the exposed skin of my neck and shoulders. "CJ, wait. What are you doing?"

"I was just checking something. Ready to head back out there?"

Are you freaking kidding me? He could have taken me right there and I wouldn't have put up a fight. Maybe it was the alcohol coursing through my body, but I was so turned on and slightly disappointed at the same time.

We returned to the dance floor hand in hand and Penelope and Reg were still dancing. I was in complete shock. The wide smile that spread across her bright red lips, and the sparkle in her emerald green eyes, spoke volumes. *I hope he doesn't hurt her.*

The entire band and Pen and I had shut down the place. As we were exiting I turned around to take a good look at the spot where Cody Jamison had teased me. The space looked even bigger as it emptied out. There were huge vaulted ceilings, with cool illuminated strung lights hanging everywhere. I hadn't noticed there was a second level full of fancy plush chairs and other upgraded décor. The bar was wrapped around the stage where they'd performed earlier and there were levels of different kinds of alcohol.

"Come on, girl," Pen said as she linked her arm through mine. "I think I might actually get to sleep with Reginald Jones," she whispered in my ear. We all climbed into the huge, fifteen-passenger van and it was like people were almost coupling up. CJ slid in beside me in the back, Reg and Penelope claimed the row in front of us. Alexis rode shotgun and Kandy sat behind the wheel, Colt was two rows back and Ambrose and some redheaded slut he'd acquired sat in the very front row. I wanted to puke every time she laughed. She sounded like those annoying dolls I had as a kid that always made a high pitched sound, even when you didn't mean to touch it.

Either way, I was sitting by Cody Jamison and felt at home. I cuddled into his arm, breathed in his strong, masculine scent and then everything went dark.

Chapter 12

She'd fallen asleep with my arm wrapped around her and she looked so innocent as she slept. She looked comfortable, like she belonged there with me. Her big brother was way up front, probably too busy finger-banging the groupie he'd picked up from the bar to notice. I rested my cheek on the top of her brown hair, and inhaled her sweet minty fragrance. She smelled so good, I wished I could eat her—but I couldn't. I was getting mixed signals from her. She seemed like she was into me, but I didn't want to push anything because I shouldn't be acting on the extreme hard-on that was growing in my pants as I held her tighter against my chest.

Fuck, I wanted this girl bad.

Reg and her friend got dropped off at his place, and Dean and the redhead were getting dropped off next. He looked back at me and shouted at me to get his little sister home safe. He trusted I wouldn't make a move, but he was so wrong. If I could have had it my way, she'd be spread eagle in my bed right now as my tongue twisted and lapped up her sweet pussy juices. I imagined how loud she'd moan and my dick was stiff as a fucking rock again. I'd be taking care of that in the shower later.

Kandy asked for Shannon's address and I told her to drop us both off there. When we arrived, Shannon was so exhausted and wasted that she was basically a fucking rag doll passed out on my chest. I hopped over the seat in front of us, ran around the back of the van and carefully slid her over the seat and out the back door. I tossed her over my shoulder, making sure to grab her keys out of her purse and opened the door to her small apartment at the end of the short walkway. I hit the lights and everything in her apartment lit up, neat and in its place and smelling like cinnamon. There were floral pillows all over the fabric-covered couch, with a similar pattern on the drapes. I wanted to laugh at the sight of all these flowers, but this definitely represented Shannon and her weird tastes. For some reason I hadn't noticed how ugly this was that night she invited Dean and me over.

I gently placed her down on the couch and removed the red pumps from her feet. She stirred a little as I propped her feet up on the couch, and I headed around the small island into the kitchen for a bottle of water. I placed two bottles on the counter and tried to find some aspirin so she wouldn't wake up with a killer hangover the next day. I hadn't been around her much, but she had mentioned she was a lightweight and I didn't want her to wake up feeling like shit.

I walked down the tight hallway and the bathroom was directly at the end of the hall. Girls always have their meds and shit in the bathroom, so that was my first stop. I flipped the switch and a bright-ass light shined on a huge mirror, blinding the holy fuck out of me. After a few blinks, I pulled the glass back and found the pills. I rarely ever get hung over, but Reg was a chronic sufferer, so I had learned how to treat them so it didn't interfere with practices.

I turned back to hear her coughing and gurgling on the couch. *Shit, I hope she doesn't puke.* I grabbed a small trash can that I saw in the bathroom and bolted down the hall. As soon as I got the can near her the puke slid right out of her mouth into it. *Fuck, that's nasty.*

I held her hair back as she violently assaulted the can. Surprisingly, her puke didn't stink, but I could be immune to the smell since Reg's tended to make a skunk's ass smell like blooming flowers on a spring day.

After she'd finished, I noticed she'd gotten a little on the top of her dress. Normally I would have bailed by now, but I couldn't do that to my best friend's little sister, not after he specifically told me to take care of her. *Fuck.*

I'd somehow gotten her to get off the couch and walk into the bathroom. I didn't feel right stripping her like this, so I asked her to take her dress off and lie in the tub with a towel draped over her body. As the dated tub filled up, my hard-on returned as the dry towel was now damp and clinging to her curvy body. *Fuck.*

"Shan, can you wash yourself?"

She gurgled some weird-ass response and I took that as a big fat no. *Of course.* Her head flopped back on some pillow thing she had attached to the back of the tub and her hands fell by her side into the water. *Fuck me.*

I quickly washed her off without even sneaking a peek and got her out of the tub. She had a robe behind her door and I wrapped her up in it. At this point modesty was out the fucking window. I saw what I saw, and there was no fucking way I'd un-see it. *Not that I'm complaining.*

Her room was beside the bathroom and she'd managed to sober up enough to climb onto her bed. I ran back down the hall to get the water and aspirin. I didn't want any more damage to happen to this girl. She'd already puked half her guts out.

Before I made it back to the room I heard a high-pitched shriek. *What in the ever-loving fuck?* I booked it as fast as I could back to her room to see her standing beside the bed, tightly gripping the robe around her body.

"Oh my God, CJ? Thank God. How did I get here? I don't remember anything after the club."

"You passed out. I carried you in and put you on the couch, but you puked your guts out and got some on your dress, so I—uh—had to wash you up. Don't worry, I didn't cop a feel—scout's honor." I raised my right hand and crossed my two fingers, trying to stifle a laugh.

Her cheeks were flushed with embarrassment and I thought it was kind of cute. She had nothing I hadn't seen or been in before, but hers was going to be a little harder to get.

"CJ, can you please get out of my room? I'm so embarrassed. I don't even know what to say."

"Thanks would be nice. I could have let you choke on your own vomit, ya know."

"Thanks? Can you get out please, I'm soaking wet and want to put some clothes on."

"Here, make sure to take these. I'll go crash on the couch."

I respected her wishes and headed toward the living room. I could hear her yelling at herself for being so stupid and it made me laugh my ass off. I grabbed my phone out of my pocket and had several texts. One from this broad I was supposed to fuck tonight—delete. One was from Dean, asking if his sister was all right. He should have been fucking the broad he brought home, not giving me the third degree about his damn sister.

I went back into the small living space and cleaned up the mess she'd made before our little bathroom fiasco. As I was about to plant my ass on the larger couch, she came down the hallway covered in an oversized gray hoody and sweat pants. "A little much, given the prior circumstances, don't you think?"

"Shut up, CJ. I'm already embarrassed you had to bathe the puke residue off my half-naked body. Can we not make this any more awkward?"

"Deal. So you got anything to eat around here? You need to eat something greasy before you wake up feeling worse tomorrow than you do right now."

"I have some turkey burgers in the freezer."

"Gross. Do you have a Chinese food joint or something around here?"

"CJ, it's after two in the morning."

"And? There's got to be something open. Let me use your laptop."

In a matter of minutes, I found a Chinese food place that was open until four a.m. and they fucking delivered. I ordered fried rice and some type of chicken.

"CJ, you really didn't have to do that. I'm a big girl, I can handle myself."

I pointed to the trash can. "Really, now?"

"Okay, well, most of the time I can."

"Shan, when's the last time you let someone take care of you?" Her eyes gravitated to the floor, completely avoiding direct contact with mine. "That's what I thought. I'm pretty sure you're always taking care of other people. It's nice to let go once in a fucking while, ya know?"

"It's hard. I'm a control freak. I have everything planned down to the very last intricate detail."

"And that's no way to live. You sound like my ninety-year-old grandma right now." Her brown eyes cut over to me like daggers, but she scrunched her nose up like a fucking rabbit and it made me laugh.

"What?"

"You're cute when you're trying to act pissed."

"Whatever, CJ!" The doorbell rang and I motioned for her to stay put. "I'll get it. Sit your ass right where you are."

A short Chinese dude smiled as I opened the door. "Your order, sir."

"Thanks." I grabbed the large brown bag and tipped him.

Bumping the door shut with my foot, I asked "Do you have any paper plates or anything?"

"Yeah, they're in the cabinet above the fridge." I dropped the bag on the counter and grabbed everything from the cabinet. She had the spoons and shit in separate plastic baggies inside a bigger baggie, and the plates and napkins were all inside their original packaging.

"Shan, do you ever use these things?"

"Not often, but when I do, I reseal what I can. I know, don't judge me."

I stacked my plate high with rice, meat and sauce. I made hers, but with half the amount of food. "This good?"

"It's perfect, thank you."

After we ate, she put on some hilarious movie with Kevin Hart and the dude that does the voice of that snowman from that movie. What was that shit called? *Frozen.* Yeah that's it.

The movie had me in fucking tears. It was a great idea though, paying someone to be your best man? Shit—I wish I'd thought of it.

"So since you seem to be sobered up now, and it's seven in the morning, I think I'll head out."

"You sure? You don't have to go. I mean, if you don't want to."

The sun shone through the window and it reflected off her freckled cheeks, making her eyes look glossy and full of lust. "I'll stay a little longer, but only because you begged me to."

Chapter 13

Oh my God. Oh my God. How the—what the? That was not how I wanted to end up with him. I wanted to willingly be taking my clothes off. Ugh, that was so embarrassing.

I couldn't believe that *the* Cody Jamison had spent the night with me. Technically neither of us slept, but he was at my place, we'd stuffed our faces with Chinese food and watched movies until he had to leave for practice at noon. I don't know how the heck he does it. I'd be passed out flat on my face if I pulled all-nighters like that. But, since he's trying to become a rock star, he already has the vampire lifestyle down pat.

I watched as he walked down the street with his muscular arms loosely flexed as he slid his hands into his pockets. My eyelids felt so heavy that I decided to crawl into bed and take a nap.

I woke up to my phone buzzing like crazy on the nightstand and my doorbell ringing like a crazy person was outside. I grabbed my phone and saw Penelope's face illuminated on my screen. "Hello?"

"Bitch, what are you doing? I haven't heard from you since last night. I thought you were dead, or kidnapped or some shit. Are you home? Open the damn door. I have wine!"

I looked down and realized I had the same sweat suit on from earlier. I slipped out of it, and slid on some black yoga pants and a pink tank, before running down the hall to the door.

"Hey."

"Hey," she said, sticking her head in and searching the place. "You all right?"

"Yeah, why?"

"Well, you're breathing kind of hard, your cheeks are flushed, and you have that thoroughly fucked look on your face."

I couldn't help but laugh, wishing it were true, but getting to hang out with CJ had almost felt as good as I imagine having sex with him would have been. "None of that happened, even though I wish it did. But enough about me, how was Reg?" Her cheerful smile quickly turned into one full of sadness and hurt. "What's wrong?"

"I need a drink first." She blew past me, heading straight into the kitchen to grab the wine glasses. She saw the paper plates and cutlery on the counter and shot me a strange look.

"What?"

"You never leave your kitchen a mess like this; was someone here with you last night?"

"So, how about that wine?" I quickly grabbed the bottle opener out of the drawer and popped open our favorite white d'Asti. I filled our glasses up and brought the opened bottle to the glass coffee table in the living room. I'd placed all my family pictures on the bottom when CJ was over, so they wouldn't get destroyed while we were eating and watching movies.

She sat down on the loveseat and I sat beside her. "Well?"

She took a huge gulp of the white, bubbly liquid. "Well, he was everything I could have imagined and more in the sack."

"Okay—so what's wrong?"

"We were so caught up in the moment and he made me feel so good, that I didn't notice he didn't put a condom on."

"Oh my God, Pen. You never let that happen!"

"I know, but it was just—different with him."

"Pen, you know he's heavy into drugs—what if?"

Her head hung low and she pulled her legs up toward her chest, wrapping her arms around her knees, and clutched the wine glass beside them and I felt so bad. "I know. I was acting like a stupid drunk groupie last night. But I can't explain it, Shan, he was different than normal."

"Different how?"

"Well, I do think he might have been high on something, but he cherished my body. Like—he took his time with me, made sure I was pleased first. I thought for sure we were gonna have headboard-banging sex, but he was so attentive to my needs. I almost felt like we were falling in love with each other."

"That's good, right? I mean, you've been into him for a while."

"Yeah, but he's always ignored me, or usually walked by me without taking a second glance, so I'm so fucking confused right now." She gulped the rest of her wine and placed the glass back on the coffee table.

"Men are freaking weird."

"And complicated," she added. "So what happened here?" She pointed at the mess on the island. *Crap. I thought we were over that.*

"Well, CJ and I—"

"Wait, Cody was here?"

"Yes, but it's not what you think."

"What am I supposed to think? He's fucking gorgeous. Please tell me you got some."

"No, but I embarrassed myself though." She refilled our glasses and grabbed a chicken wing out the box that I'd left on the table.

"Do tell."

After I filled Pen in on everything that happened, it cheered her up a little. I still wish her and Reg could connect when they weren't drunk or high, though. Hopefully he'd come around.

"So, are you going to their show tomorrow night? They're supposed to be performing at The Adonis."

"I don't know. I don't want to end up a drunken

embarrassment again."

"Shan, please. You're as innocent as they come. It was a onetime mistake, and hopefully, the next time you get CJ over here you can dust out those cobwebs."

"Shut up!" But, I kind of hoped I could. Those old feelings had returned in full force and I knew he had them too. Or at least I hoped.

"The Adonis is a huge venue and a lot of talent scouts show up there, so we might bear witness to history in the making."

That's what I'm afraid of.

Chapter 14

Cody

"Dude, we're playing at the fucking Adonis tonight, I am so fucking amped right now. I need to go and hit something before we go on."

"Reg, are you for fucking real? You're gonna do a line right now? An hour before showtime?"

"Why not?"

"Because there might be scouts there, ass-face. You get high before this show and I'm gonna put my size twelve up your ass," Dean barked.

"Bring it, tough guy." Reg shook his fist, egging him on, but Dean left the room. Most of the time Dean was all bark and no bite, but I don't take his walking away for weakness. I saw him break a guy's nose with one fucking shot at a nightclub a few weeks back.

Reg retreated upstairs, leaving me, Colt, and Alexis twiddling our thumbs on the couch until Kandy arrived with Lucy. That's what we named our pimp mobile.

"Hope you boys are ready, this might be the big break we need to make it." Alexis' eyes were round with excitement as she grabbed her purse.

I'm ready; I just hope the rest of these dicks were.

"Coming to the stage is Spasm! Give them a traditional

Adonis welcome!" Josh, the host of the night, said.

The crowd cheered their asses off for us before we even played a single note and I felt that shit coursing through my veins. I got a natural high off the crowd's energy and this one was already phenomenal.

I glanced over at each of my band members and they all gave me a head nod, before I started my riff and put my lips up to the microphone.

Take a deep breath — inhale
Let go of all the bullshit — exhale
Da de da, Da de da
Can you feel that?
In the air, in the air?
The lights casting down, turning colors, hear the sound
That's the end, that's the end
Constricting my lungs, the pain you have caused, I felt at
a loss — because of you
Because of you
Have my life feeling blue
But now it's done, it's gone so fast, your hold did not last
Constricting my lungs, the pain you have caused, I felt at
a loss — fuck you
Fuck you

I started the song and Alexis and Dean joined in. Reg beat the fuck out of the drums, while Colt's fingers made magic on the keyboard. When the last line of Breathe finished and the set ended, the crowd's energy was completely different from earlier. They were all on their feet, girls were throwing panties and I swore I saw a few pairs of boxers fly toward Red. Josh came out and he was at a loss for words. He shook our hands and then pointed to a lady standing at the bottom of the stage. Her smile was beaming and she looked overly excited to see us.

I had no idea who the hell she was, but I hoped she was someone important and not another person giving us false hope and feeding us more bullshit.

She waved to us to follow her and led us to the back into a small room with a gold star on the door.

"Have a seat, have a seat!" Now that I'd gotten a good look at her she was kind of hot. Tall, in an all white suit, with her blonde hair pulled back. She removed her coat and her tight shirt hugged her big tits and I felt my dick twitch in my pants.

"And you are?" Dean asked as we all sat at a long rectangular table across from her.

"Where are my manners? My name is Anna and I work with Thomas' Upstream Radio."

"Wait, y'all do those podcasts featuring indie music and aspiring musicians, right?" Colt asked.

"Correct. I'm glad you've heard of us. How would you guys like to come on for an interview? Maybe we can find you guys a broader audience, and maybe, just maybe, some scouts will reach out. I haven't heard raw talent like this in ages. The fact that you guys aren't signed yet is astonishing."

Hearing her say that was like adding another notch to my belt. I knew we were fucking ready for the real deal, and maybe this podcast was the first step to the road to fame.

"Welcome to Joe and Ron in the morning on Upstream Chat. We have this lovely new band here by the name of Spasm and from what we've heard, they're an up-and-coming rock band with an edge. Introduce yourselves to the audience, guys. I know it may be a little different than what you're used to, but you'll get to hear them talk back later."

"Well, I'm Ambrose, the co-founder of Spasm. This ball of fun next to me is the other co-founder, Cody. He's our badass lead guitarist, by the way. We have Alexis, also known as Red, she's hot and has a unique set of pipes. She also keeps our asses in line. That guy over there is my boy Reg, the only drummer with certified hands, and that's Colt, our resident pretty-boy keyboardist."

"Nice to meet everyone. I'm Joe and that's Ron. Now how did you all meet? And how did you come up with the name Spasm?"

"Oh God, well, Ambrose and I were friends back in the day. I came back to town, saw his flyer for band auditions and tried out. Alexis and I got recruited on the same day, she told us about Reg, and pretty boy here was just an added bonus in disguise. Alexis was honestly a true blessing, because she can play instruments too, and Ambrose heard that special something in her voice and knew she'd give us that unique and awesome sound we were looking for. And as for the name . . . it was a joke. We're always calling each other spazzes and we knew what we wanted our fans to feel when we performed and poof—Spasm was born!"

"That's awesome. Well, enough about the back story, what have you guys currently been working on? Anything new?"

"I guess it's time to put up or shut up, huh? Alexis, you wanna start us off?"

"With what song?"

"Your choice, sweet pea."

"Don't worry, guys and madam, sing whatever you want, this is a satellite radio show so vulgar language is welcome! It'll be edited for replay later," Joe said.

The writing is on the wall
The tears they seem to fall
Bad shit I can't recall
But I'm taking it out on you
Taking it out on you
It's hard to bring myself back from the brink
One step closer to that drink
Escaping from reality with the burning fluid on my gums
It burns, it turns
Sometimes I don't know why it makes me numb

But it feels better than you
It tastes better than you
It conceals better than you
Yes, I'm taking it out on you
Taking it out on you

"We haven't quite finished it yet, but that's a current piece written by yours truly," I gloated.

"Wow, you guys! The lights are flashing non-stop. Let's take a few calls, shall we?"

"Sure."

"You're on the air with Joe and Ron, what did you think about Spasm's song?"

Inaudible yelps were blaring through the speaker, followed by a loud horn beeping.

"Hello?"

"Hi, sorry—I just. I never get through and just—you guys are freaking—wow!"

"What's your name and where you calling from?"

"I'm Sally from Andover, Mass."

"Well, Sally, it's obvious you approve of our new friends too, right?"

"Absolutely! I've never heard a sound like that before! You guys performed flawlessly, even when put on the spot. That's so rare, and I hope the scouts are on the lines because you guys should be snatched up soon!"

"Thanks, Sally. Let's take another call. You're on the air with Joe, Ron, and Spasm."

"Oh my fucking God! You guys rock, and Alexis, your voice is angelic with a hint of sweetness and spice. I bet you're hot, too."

Red's cheeks turned crimson as she heard the guy hitting on her through the speakers. I know she wasn't interested, but she never refused a compliment. "Thank you."

"Hello, you're on the air."

"Hi, this is Simon Kenmore from ACD Records. We'd love to speak with you off-air, if that's possible."

"We'll put you on hold. And there you have it folks, three calls in and the scouts are already chomping at the bit. Let's wish our new friends Spasm good luck!"

"That was a killer fucking experience. Three scouts wanted to talk to us. I'm still in shock, man. Talk about a major ego boost."

"I know, but we don't want to get too fucking eager, either. We're not gonna accept the very first offer that comes our way, because no matter what, our music is always number one and no one is gonna change that. I don't care how much money they throw at us," Colt snapped.

"I know, but still. That show can make or break people and I can feel we're heading in the right direction."

"Well, let's get off our asses and head over to ACD Records and see what Simon has to say first," Dean said.

"Colt, call your bitch so we can roll out."

"Screw you, Reg. She's not a bitch! And she's already outside." He laughed.

We all headed down to the van and I felt like my balls had grown twice as big because my strides became slower and more powerful. *We got this.*

Chapter 15

"Ms. Moore, have you come up with a topic for your article yet? You told me you were working on a magazine piece, but didn't relay what type. Is it an exposé? A how-to? An opinion article? What?" Professor Williams asked.

"I was thinking of doing a profile and interview article, but I'm not sure yet."

"Well, whatever you decide, it's due in two weeks, and it better blow me away, Ms. Moore. In this industry you can get swallowed alive before you've made a dent in it."

"That's okay, Shannon. I'll get you a job fetching me coffee and doughnuts when I make it," Ashley tittered behind me.

I couldn't stand her, she was always bothering me and bragging about how much better she was at writing than I was. I had better things to do with my time, than to fight with a snooty tramp.

She clicked by in her fancy, high-dollar heels, short mini skirt, and tight cashmere sweater and knocked my papers off my desk. "Oops." She swung her golden locks over her shoulder and kept walking.

Such a witch.

Thankfully this was my last class for the week and I could escape and hang out with Penelope for the weekend.

> **Me:** *I have my things in the car, I'm coming over asap!*
>
> **Pen:** *Let me guess, plastic Patty again?*

Me: *You know it.*

Pen: *Get your ass over here and bring some chicken from Cappy's!*

I pulled up in front of Penelope's apartment and she was already sitting on the porch waiting for me. As I pushed the button to open the trunk, she ran down the steps to help me. "Hey, you have the food, right?"

"Of course, and before you ask, the wine's in there, too."

"You're such a great friend!"

She snatched my large suitcase from the shallow trunk and the bucket of chicken, while I grabbed the rest of my belongings and extras. I slammed the trunk lid to my Taurus and followed her up the short stone steps and into her small one-bedroom apartment.

I placed the food and wine down on the wooden coffee table and brought my bags into her room. She had a huge, king-sized bed, with some kind of magic memory foam on it that felt like I was sleeping on a cloud. Her closet was also huge, but the rest of the space was pretty tight.

I washed my hands in the bathroom and joined her back in the living room. "Oh my God, this chicken is the balls, girl. I swear they put crack in this stuff."

"Probably, I bet it's the top secret spice they add." We both chuckled loudly. She laughed so hard she started coughing and then ran off to the kitchen sink and puked in it. "Dude, are you okay?"

"Yeah, a little piece slid down the wrong way, that's all!" Her voice sounded a little strange, but I chalked it up to choking.

"Okay, well let's open this wine and get this party started."

"Of course. Hey, did you hear the Upstream podcast this morning?"

"No. I missed it. Who was on it?"

"Spasm! They played this new sample called The Writing's on the Wall or some shit. It was so good! A scout called into the show and Reg told me two more called off the air and they were going to see them all this weekend!"

"That's so cool. They're about to blow up I can feel it! And wow... *Reg* told you?"

"Yeah, I think I finally wore him down. Guess you'd better give Cody the goods now, so you'll be repellent for all those thirsty bitches he'll attract on the road."

I hadn't thought of that. I liked him so much, but what if sleeping with him made things worse? What if it had the opposite effect and he craved more than what I could give him?

Pen and I listened to the podcast replay, stuffed our faces, got drunk off our asses and were on our way to bed. I don't know what made me do it, but I decided to text CJ.

> **Me:**   I heard about the scouts, good luck!
>
> **CJ:**   Isn't it past ur bedtime? And thanks haha.
>
> **Me:**   Shut up! No it's not, but I was just thinking of you.
>
> **CJ:**   What were u thinking about doing to me? ;)

Omg what am I doing? Shut up, Shannon.

> **Me:**   Nothing!
>
> **CJ:**   Sure... Let's hang out after the show tomorrow. Pen already has the address ;)
>
> **Me:**   Deal.

"How do I look?"

"Like a million bucks, Pen. Seriously, I envy your shape so much."

"Shut up, you have a killer ass, and you also have those cute little freckles all over. Guys dig that shit. Hell, if you weren't my best friend, I'd hit it."

I could feel my cheeks flush with embarrassment. She knew

how bashful I got when people complimented me, even her.

"I think we both look extra-fuckable tonight. I plan on having round two with Reg, if he doesn't act like a dick again."

"Good luck, I—uh—have a date with CJ."

"What? Little Ms. Prim and Proper has a date? In that case, let me do your hair and makeup!"

After an hour of hot tools yanking my scalp and seemingly endless plucking and pampering to my face, we were finally heading out the door. Pen ordered us a car for the night because she told me she planned on getting white-girl wasted and didn't want either of us driving.

The black Town Car was waiting outside for us and as we entered the back and slid across the smooth leather, I felt butterflies in my stomach. "What's wrong, Shan? You seem tense," she asked, crossing her bare leg over mine.

"I just—really like him, you know? I didn't think all of those feelings from before would come back so quickly. And I don't think I can really handle the rock star scene. Going to a few shows is nice, but I can't do this, not all the time. I feel like I'd drag him down."

"Shan, you're not marrying the guy—relax. You're allowed to have some fun with a hot guy; it's Cody Jamison, for Pete's sake!" She pulled a small flask out of her purse and handed it to me. "Here. Drink this, it'll calm you down."

I took a swig and the clear liquid immediately burned my throat on the way down. "What was that?"

"Vodka. Take another sip." She pushed the flask back up to my lips and I reluctantly obliged.

We pulled up in front of a huge building with a neon sign that read *Slade's* above the entrance. I had heard a lot about this place, but I'd never actually been inside before. The exterior was covered with bricks, with beautiful square windows lined in a silver trim. I could hear the live music booming through the doors. Inside, there were people everywhere dancing, drinking, and lounging on the long, purple couches. Security was in full force and it actually made me feel safe. The floors were wooden, smooth and polished without a single scratch on them. A huge crystal chandelier dangled over the dance floor with colorful lights inside, splashing all the colors of the rainbow. There was a fifty-dollar cover fee that night, but since Spasm was playing, they already had our entry covered. We were immediately seated in the VIP section of the club on the second floor, away from the crowds, and there was a large bottle of Pinot Noir in a bucket full of ice, with two huge wine glasses beside it. Penelope held one in her hand and kissed it. "I wish I had this thing at home! I might have to bring it with me."

"You're a mess, girl!"

She popped the top and filled our glasses up halfway. I heard Alexis in the background and we both turned our attention to the band on the stage that was surrounded by a huge swarm of people below. Looking at CJ on stage almost took my breath away. The rips in his denim jeans were strategically placed, the black tank fitted his body like a glove and he actually put some effort in styling his chestnut brown hair.

"This is one of my favorite songs, and if there's anyone out there that has been hurt by a fucking liar, this one is for you!"

Liar

Liar

The lies that spew from inside of you, you took it all and damaged me

Ripping my heart from my chest, I believed you

You loved me,

You needed me,

Deceived me,

I stayed

You meant it,

You hated me,

You cheated,

I prayed

Continued to believe we were meant to be,

I was so naïve,
I was so naïve
The bruises under my sleeve embarrassed me
Not anymore, I'm going through the door – forever
Get me out of this mess, the scars on my chest, are
reminders of the life I'll leave behind
You say you love
You begged for more,
But the blood I spilt will be no more
Fuck you,
Stay away from me,
Shut up,
I won't take anymore
Fuck this,
You lying sack of shit,
The truth has set me free
Get away from me, stay away from me
Liar
You fucking liar, your charm once captivated my heart
But you broke it in two, and I hate you
No more tears to be shed, no more blood to be bled
No more bones to be broken, no more pain for the taken
I won't take you in; you're full of fucking sin
You liar, you're a fucking liar,
I'm done with you
Drain me no more; you're lying on the floor
Feel the need to bleed,
No more reason to breathe,
You fucking animal
Perish into the darkness, go into the light
I won't be seeing you anymore – goodnight

I won't take this anymore, why must you do this to me?

You suck the life out of me, I can't take this anymore

I always stay when I should leave, I've taken too much time to grieve

Not any more, I'm getting stronger and it's not because of you

Fuck you. I'm gone, never to fall into this trap you've caused

I won't take this anymore

I won't take this anymore

I never got what I wanted; I never got what I needed

I've set myself free, please let go of me

Please let go of me

I'm stronger than I used to be

I swear every single woman in the building was on their feet. I felt every lyric she sang deep down in my core. That was true every time she sang, but this song I felt like it was written just for me. My ex was abusive, and of course I stayed because I was young and dumb. Eventually I got away, but not without a lot of psychological damage, and I think that's why it's hard for me to trust people. Sure I've dated, and had sex, but I want more than that; I'm sure every woman does. As Alexis sang, I couldn't keep my eyes off CJ. His fingers were making love to his fret board and his deep raspy voice sounded magical over the speakers.

"That song was so fucking real!" Pen yelled over the crowd's cheers. I swore I saw her wipe a stray tear away.

"I know!" I could feel the goose bumps on my arms from the performance. I looked down at CJ from the balcony and I'm not sure if he actually saw me or not, but I felt like his eyes locked with mine from below. He whispered to Ambrose and pointed toward us. *Crap, he did see me.* "Let's not let this Pinot go to waste!" I said to Pen.

"Bottoms up!" She clinked her glass against mine, and we

sucked every last drop out of the bottle before Spasm made their way up to greet us.

The bouncer let the band in with all of their equipment, and CJ walked right over to me.

"Hey."

"Hey." My legs shook as he placed his hand down on my thigh, rubbing it up and down as he sat down beside me. He smelled like an outdoor spring and I wanted to bathe in his scent. Amazingly, he didn't break a single sweat during his performance.

"How are you?" he asked genuinely. His lips turned up at the corners and his eyes slightly sparkled.

"Good, your performance was awesome!" *Calm down, Shan, you're acting like a groupie.*

"Thanks, but enough about the band, let's go somewhere a little more *quiet.*"

He took my hand and led me past the other members. "Hey, where do you think you two are going?" Ambrose asked. *Crap, he's onto us.*

"Dude, I just wanted to buy the lady a drink, chill out."

"One drink. If you hurt her again, CJ, I'll kill you!"

"Dude, chill."

"Shut up, Ambrose. I'm not ten anymore. It's just a drink and I am a grown woman."

"You're still my little sis, and sorry if I'm on edge, but after the last asshole you introduced me to . . ." he paused to show the old scars on his knuckles. "If I ever see him again, I will end his life—just sayin.'"

CJ led me down the spiral staircase and back onto the first floor. We found a room down the hall that was away from all the noise and not nearly as crowded. It felt more private and comfortable. There was a small bar in the back of the room and CJ sat me down on the plush couch as he went over and ordered our drinks. Things were getting a little hazy and I hoped I didn't embarrass myself again by drinking too much.

As he strode back to me, heat flared from in between my thighs. It'd been a while since I'd had sex and my body was quickly reminding me of the deep attraction I had to Cody Jamison. He shot me his infamous smirk and I almost melted on the spot.

"Someone will be over with our drinks shortly. So what did you *really* think about the performance tonight?" He inched closer to me on the couch and his fingers lightly brushed the hem of my dress.

"Um, it was really good. I love when Alexis leads, especially with something as powerful as "Liar." It really touches a spot deep down in my soul, makes me feel invincible."

"Good to know. Well, I'll let you in on a little secret, we've written three more songs and I hope you can come to our practice tomorrow at Reg's so you can hear them and give me your honest opinion. You keep shit real with me, Shan. I really appreciate that about you."

Omg he wants to know what I think about his music? I think the alcohol in my system was causing my brain to malfunction and overreact. "Well, I like things about you too; just wish I could get to know you better. Get to know *this* CJ." *Crap, did I just say that out loud?*

"Here are your drinks, sir." The waiter handed CJ a glass of amber liquid, whiskey I assume, and handed me a fruity frozen drink with a purple umbrella and a fruit kabob. I took a sip and it tasted like paradise. I tried to inhale it and a pain struck me in the head.

"Owwwwww!"

"Slow down, killer. You're not invincible to brain freeze." He laughed. His voice was raspy and deep. I wish his laugh would never stop.

I rubbed my temples for a moment, and then slowly sipped paradise again. I uncrossed my legs, then slowly re-crossed them, as he watched my every move. "Shannon, I'm not gonna beat around the fucking bush. I want you. There are things I'd like to do to you, that you probably wouldn't be able to handle."

In shock, I slouched back on the couch, mouth agape, trying to find the words to say, but I froze. He slid closer to me and ran his fingers over my thighs, discreetly lifting the cotton material as he bunched it up on my lap. His fingers grazed the inside of my thigh, and then swiped across the lace material covering my mound and I suddenly tensed. "CJ—"

"Tell me no, and I'll stop, Shannon." His eyes darkened with desire as he carefully searched mine for a response. "Good, don't move."

His fingers carefully pushed the material to the side and he slowly massaged my clit with his thumb. I almost forgot where we were for a moment and then panicked at the thought of someone catching us. "CJ, wait."

He nipped at my neck with his teeth, and growled in my ear. "Tell me you want me to stop, Shan. Tell me." One finger dipped in and I was crumbling at the seams. He dipped another inside and I came undone. My muscles contracted around his fingers, squeezing them as he rubbed the tiny bud inside, completely sending me over the edge.

What I felt was a state of euphoria as he fixed my clothes and sucked his fingers.

"Mmm, just as sweet as I thought you'd taste. Let's go and rejoin the band before they get suspicious."

"I'll m-meet up with you in a minute; I have to go to the bathroom." I needed a timeout; there was no way I could return to the group like this. Pen would notice something had changed before I'd even set foot back into the VIP.

The bathroom was unbelievably gorgeous. There was a small water fountain in the middle with colorful lights reflecting in the water, and a plush couch directly at the entrance. I'm assuming that's for the nights when it's really busy and there's a line for miles. Each stall was large and spotless. No signs of toilet paper, trash or anything in sight. It smelled like lavender and had a calming effect on me, or that was my excuse, anyway. After the orgasm he'd just given me, I'm not sure I'd be able to remain calm around him ever again.

There were huge vanity mirrors with seats to touch up your

makeup and sinks with large mirrors above to fix other things. Every piece of tile was intact and the watercolor paintings on the wall were gorgeous. *I wish my bathroom looked like this.*

I exited the lush bathroom and heard a group of girls cackling like hens. They were all surrounding CJ, and of course I felt a tinge of fire burn within. *After letting my guard down with him, of course he'd be attracting more girls the moment I stepped away. I'm such an idiot.*

He saw me out the corner of his eye, and quickly dismissed the club groupies. "What was that all about?" I asked, jealousy leaking into my voice.

"Nothing, they just wanted my autograph. After I signed they refused to leave until you showed up. I told them you were my future baby mama and they split."

"Wow, already using me as bitch repellent—nice."

"Shan, it's cute when you swear. I don't think I've heard much of it before, but I hope to hear it again, preferably while I'm burying my cock deep inside of you."

At that moment, I wish we could have left so I could feel him deep inside of me, but he grabbed my hand, placed a kiss on the top, and led me out the door. *In due time, Shannon, in due time.*

We walked back up the stairs to rejoin the party, but Ambrose was missing. Pen shot me a weird look, shrugged her shoulders and then smiled at me. I mouthed the words "No," but she laughed. She wouldn't believe anything I'd tell her right now anyway. I could feel my face turning beet red, and the wetness between my legs remained, even though I tried to clean myself up in the bathroom. I craved more—so much more.

Chapter 16

Shannon was putty in my hands. I didn't think I was capable of wanting to fuck someone so badly, until I reconnected with her. The fact that she was off-limits made it all so much sweeter. I would have taken her on the couch downstairs if I hadn't thought we'd end up on a website somewhere. Plus, Dean was probably floating around somewhere, searching for us. I could feel it. He was overprotective as fuck when it came to her. I didn't blame him though. She was so innocent, and it would be easy for her to be manipulated by the wrong person. *Someone that wasn't me.*

The expression on her face when she came on my fingers replayed over and over in my head. Her nipples were like little pebbles pressing against her dress, her lip curled when she was close, and her eyes rolled when her body seized. My cock twitched behind my zipper. I needed to get away from her before I snatched her into a stall and plowed into her sweet pussy until she couldn't walk. *Fuck.*

"Cody. Earth to fucking Cody! Cody Jamison!"

"What, man, what?"

"Are you all right? You've been in a trance for like half an hour, bro."

"Colt, I'm good. I'm just thinking about our performance. We fucking killed earlier."

"Yeah we did, but I've known you for a while now and I can definitely see the wheels are turning about something else.

Come and grab a drink with me. Kandy, I'll be right back, hon," he said, as he kissed her on the cheek.

I followed him downstairs and I shit you not, we ended up in the same room I finger-banged Shannon in. I looked over at the couch and tried to stifle a laugh.

"Whiskey on the rocks?"

"You know it. Have one with me."

"Oh, I planned on it."

He paid for two rounds of drinks and as we went to find a seat, I led him away from the finger-bang couch.

"So," he said, as he took a bitch-like sip of whiskey.

"So."

"What's going on with you and Shannon?"

"Nothing."

"Dude, you know you can tell me, I'm not Ambrose. I can see there's something going on between the two of you."

"She's cool, bro."

"You bang her yet?"

"Nah. I want to though."

"What's stopping you?"

"I don't fucking know. If it were any other girl I would have had her in all positions, and in all holes. But with her, I actually want to wait because I know it'll fucking be worth it."

"Well fuck, Cody Jamison is actually taking it slow for a change. Is your dick okay?" He laughed.

"Fuck no, and fuck you for asking!" I laughed, then chugged the two glasses in front of me.

The venue was shutting down and we were all being kicked out—literally. We were the last ones in the VIP section with a couple of groupies mixed in. We tossed our equipment and instruments in the back of the van and all piled up inside. Shannon and her friend didn't join us this time. I guess they had their own car or some shit. I guess it was for the best, because the way my dick hurt right now, I wouldn't have been able to control myself once I got inside her panties.

A horny blonde sat beside me, and ran her hands all over my junk. I almost grabbed the back of her neck and pushed her face down on my cock, but I refrained. *What the fuck is wrong with me?*

Reg invited me to chill at his house for the night, and two girls accompanied us: the desperate blonde from the van, and some drunk redhead that refused to get out anywhere else. He let them inside and I went downstairs. "I need to shower," I shouted up the stairs.

"Can I come with?" begged the blonde.

"No thanks." She pouted her lips like a kid who was just scolded by their mom.

I grabbed my sweats and a tank from the downstairs closet and as I went into the bathroom I made sure I locked the door and put the chair in front of the knob, just in case these bitches were psycho.

I turned the water on as hot as I could possibly stand it and stepped in. The water ran from the back of my neck, down the crack of my ass, all the way down to my feet. Soothing everything it touched, except my cock. I thought of the finger-banging session I had on the couch with Shannon and slid my hand as fast as I could over the head and down the shaft of my cock. I placed my free hand against the shower, bracing myself for the explosive nut I felt was about to be released. My body tensed as the hot liquid flew out of the tip and ricocheted off the tile. *Fuck.*

After toweling myself off and tossing my clothes on, I heard a shit-ton of banging upstairs and high-pitched screaming.

"Oh my God, is he dead? Oh God, oh God!" I heard as I bolted up the stairs.

"What the fuck happened?" Reg was face down on the carpet and his body was convulsing. I turned him on his side and foam spewed from his mouth, his eyes rolling in the back of his head. "Reg? What the fuck dude? Can one of you bitches call 911? I'd like my friend to live tonight!"

After listening to the dispatcher's instructions over the phone, the ambulance finally arrived and carefully loaded him on the stretcher. "Fuck, is he gonna be okay?"

The paramedic made a face and answered, "I hope so, will anyone be accompanying us?"

"I will, I'm his brother," I lied. "Can you bitches let yourselves out without stealing his shit?"

"That won't be necessary, Cody. I'm here! I got your text and got here as fast as I could," Colt said.

"Thank God, man. I don't know what the fuck happened. I came out of the shower and heard all this banging and screaming. Not the good kind either."

I grabbed my vest and followed the guys into the back of the ambulance. They were working on Reg, trying to get his breathing stabilized. After the seizure it was like his body was struggling to take a breath. It took a lot to scare me, but this absolutely did.

"What the heck is going on?"

I walked across the street and found my friend Jensen on the ground, beaten within an inch of his life. He'd gotten hit so hard that his body started shaking and his eyes were rolling in the back of his head. I told him not to mess with the older kids, but he was a magnet for bullies. He was only fifteen, like me, only I wasn't as stupid as he was. I'd never mess with the Argyle street kids.

Jensen was the complete opposite of me. He wore thick frames on his face, his blond hair was in a bowl cut and he always wore whatever his mom brought home from the thrift shop. No matter what though, he wouldn't back down from a fight, and I did admire him for his bravery.

I yelled at Scott to keep his head to the side while I went to find his mom. She was a nurse and I knew she'd know what to do. He'd probably be punished for the rest of his life, but I wanted to make sure he lived to hear her bitch him out about it.

I ran across the road and knocked on the big red door as fast as I could. Mrs. Jensen took one look at me and grabbed her leather med bag from underneath the table. "Where is he?" I pointed across the street and she flew down the stairs after noticing her son was lying almost lifeless on the ground.

"Willy? Willy? What happened?"

"He was fighting with the Argyle street kids again."

"Ugh, those kids are a bunch of arseholes! I wish they'd pick on someone their own size and not me baby." She wiped the puke from his lips and he seemed okay, besides a few bruises on the right side of his face. "Willy, what's going on with you? You know you have epilepsy! You could have died trying to take on those jerks!"

"I'm sorry, mum, but they were saying they wanted to do horrible things to you and I couldn't take hearing that rubbish any longer."

His mom was pretty hot—short red hair, with big boobs and a big butt. Her scrubs were always tight and all the boys on the block couldn't help but stare at her. She was a full-on MILF. Her Scottish accent made everything she said sound hot, too.

I kneeled beside Jensen and whispered in his ear. "Dude, you scared the crap out of me, I thought for sure you were a goner."

"Never."

His mom picked him up off the ground and put him in the back of their ancient Volvo. She took him to the emergency room after every fight to make sure he didn't have any other injuries. Poor guy. That was certainly one of the scariest things I'd ever seen.

After my impromptu trip down memory lane, they finally got Reg stabilized and into a room. He had all kinds of wires and tubes going in and out of his body. He had a tube shoved so far down his throat that I thought it was doing the opposite of helping him breathe and it freaked me the fuck out seeing him like this. I left his ass alone for thirty fucking minutes and who the fuck knows what he took.

"Is he okay?" a soft voice whispered from behind me. It was Shannon's friend Penelope.

"I don't know. I left him alone for thirty fucking minutes and found him on the floor, surrounded by stupid bitches that almost let him die."

Tears fell from her eyes as she placed her hand over her lips, trying to hide its quiver. I got up and waved her over, pulling her into my side for a hug. "He'll be all right. This is fucking indestructible Reg. But I need you to promise me something, Pen."

"What? What is it?"

"When he gets through this, and goes through the withdrawals, I need your help. I can't watch it anymore. It fucks with my head seeing him go through it. It'll suck, but I know you can handle it. He likes you, you know. He's just being an ass because he's scared of the 'c' word."

"Cancer?"

"Commitment."

She stifled a laugh and took a seat beside him. She placed her hand on his chest and whispered something in his ear, before returning her gaze to me. "Hey, Cody?"

"Yeah?" I said, walking over.

"Here's my address, you should go and keep Shan company." She winked as she placed the small ripped paper in my hands. "Now get out of here. I'll make sure I update you if anything changes."

I hailed a cab to Penelope's place and the light was still on in the living room. I normally didn't get nervous about surprising a chick, but my stomach flipped as I walked up the stairs and knocked on the door.

"Hello?" I heard as she slightly cracked the door.

"Hey."

"CJ?" She unlatched the chain off the door and let me in.

"What are you doing here?" She tightly clasped her robe together in her hand, embarrassment flushing through her cheeks.

"Your friend gave me a break from Reg duty, and told me to come over here and keep you company."

"Why would she do that? I'm fine."

"That you are, Shannon."

I took a step forward, closing the distance between us. I carefully tilted her chin up with my finger, and placed my lips against hers. Thoughts of the club flashed through my mind and I had to feel her. I couldn't play games any longer. *She was fine now, but she would be fan-fucking-tastic when I was done with her.*

I pushed the robe off of her shoulders and let it slide to the ground, pausing to admire the lace set she had hidden underneath. I nipped at her neck with my teeth, marking my territory. "Not so hard, CJ."

Yes, harder CJ. I pushed her back against the wall and bore my eyes into hers. Her body shook slightly as I pressed my lips against her ear, slowly sucking the lobe in between my teeth. My hands grazed the exposed flesh beside her bra strap and slid it down either side of her arms.

Cupping her firm ass in my hands, I lifted her up into my arms, pressing her against my chest. She automatically wrapped her legs around my waist. "Where's the bedroom?"

"CJ, we cannot do this on my best friend's bed."

"Who said anything about a bed?" I smirked.

Chapter 17

When I'd heard that knock on the door, CJ was the last person I expected to see on the other side. As we made our way to the bedroom, the butterflies in my stomach were doing complete somersaults. I'd wanted this for so long and now it was really happening.

As we entered the room, he placed me down on my feet and locked the door behind us. "Just in case." His vest and shirt were off in one quick motion as he stalked toward me. His body was absolute perfection. Smooth caramel skin, tightly drawn muscles, disheveled hair, and his brown eyes were darkened. He was going to claim me even if I hadn't wanted him to.

His slightly roughened hands slid behind my back and unclasped my bra, my bottom lip retracted between my teeth as I tried to guess what he was thinking. *Did he like what he saw? Was it too much? Not enough?* I was always self-conscious about the freckles covering my body. Slightly yanking a few loose pieces of my hair, my neck snapped back as his tongue traveled from the side of my neck down to the center of my breasts. The warm heat from his mouth covered my nipple and I yelped as he pinched the stiffened peak between his teeth. His mouth traveled to the other side, repeating the same action and my panties were completely soaked.

My skin went ablaze as his tender kisses made their way to the top of the lace garment, and what he did next shocked me. The material ripped and as the pieces fell to the floor, his tongue slipped in between my wet folds and my knees almost dropped me to the ground.

My body trembled as he twisted and flicked, sucked and twirled his tongue, navigating through my folds, devouring me like I was his last meal. An intense pressure was building inside of me, one I'd never felt before. He wrapped his arms around the back of my thighs and held onto my ass as he pushed his tongue deeper inside of me.

That was it—my body betrayed me. Warmth seeped through my skin, my eyes rolled into the back of my head and I seized on his face. My breathing was erratic and every crevice on my body tingled. Pleased with himself, he placed me on the floor and his lips crashed into mine, sharing the flavor of my juices with me. Breaking the kiss, he asked, "Shannon, are you on birth control?"

"No."

"Damn." He crawled over to his jeans and pulled a condom out of his back pocket. I hadn't noticed how large he was until he placed his hand around his cock, pumping it to reach maximum girth. I don't know what came over me, but I crawled over to him, shaky legs and all, and wrapped my lips around the head. "Fuck, Shannon."

It stiffened quickly and it was huge. Thick and wide, and perfectly shaped, I was afraid all of it wouldn't fit inside of me. My eyes must have given away my inner thoughts because he looked down at me and smiled. "Don't worry, it's big I know, but it'll fit—it always fits."

I sure hope so.

Sex with Cody Jamison was everything I could have imagined and more. He was gentle at first, allowing my body to adjust to his size, and then he took everything from me. He hit places deep inside my core that had never been reached before. I'd lost count after the third orgasm as to how many I'd actually had. I don't know what he means to do with me, but I'd love to do it again. Wild, spontaneous, and addicting is how I'd describe it.

We'd both fallen asleep on the floor and I woke up first. I looked over at him still in a sex coma, with the thin sheet barely covering his nether regions, and grabbed my phone to find a few texts from Pen.

Pen: *Reg is still knocked out, but he actually looks peaceful.*

Pen: *U must be fuckin, huh? Y'all better not be getting your coochie and nut butter all over my bed.*

Me: *OMG, I'd never screw on ur bed, but I can't promise we didn't get that stuff all over ur floor ;p*

Pen: *I'm so glad he cleaned out the cobwebs. Please tell me ur together now? You 2 make me sick.*

Me: *Idk, but whatever happens happens. Keep me posted about Reg, k?*

Pen: *K.*

I placed my phone back on the charger and tried to get up, but I was so sore. *Oh my God, he really did a number on me. I hope this isn't what he does to other girls too.*

I crawled to the door, unlocking it and continued into the bathroom. My legs felt like Jell-O after the sex-a-thon we'd had. I grasped hold of the porcelain sink and the side of the toilet and pulled myself up onto the bowl. Grabbing a cloth, I ran some cool water on it and dabbed it between my legs to relieve the soreness.

After I cleaned myself up and regained partial strength in my legs, I tossed on a pair of boy shorts and a tank as he slept away on the floor. *He looks so peaceful.* I headed down the narrow hallway and into the kitchen to grab the leftover food and the unfinished bottle of wine.

I sat on the couch flipping through the channels when I heard footsteps head into the bathroom, then heard the water from the shower turn on. *Guess he's making himself at home.*

I kept my gaze focused on the TV until I heard him come out and head down the hall toward me. Out the corner of my eye, I saw a towel draped around his waist. Unable to stay focused, I glanced at him and the towel was in his hands. He towel-dried his hair and grinned at me. *Busted.* "No need to be shy now, Shannon. You've already seen everything I have." He chuckled, wrapping the towel back around his waist. Droplets of water were sliding down his toned chest. I found myself sucking my bottom lip between my teeth as a fire was relit between my thighs.

"So what do you have to eat in this place? I'm starving."

"Cold chicken, and fries. Here, help yourself." I passed him the bucket, and he grabbed a leg out, plopping down onto the couch next to me.

Coconut smells amazing on him.

CJ had disappeared sometime before the sun came up and I was thankful. I didn't want Pen to come home and find us half naked on her couch. I know she wouldn't care, but she'd never let me live it down. Just like she wouldn't let me live down the "incident."

I was still sore, but I was able to walk with a little more pep in my step that morning. I took a shower and as I conditioned my hair, the idea for my article popped into my head. *Maybe I could interview Spasm. They're on the rise to stardom, and if I was the first to break them out into the tabloids, I'd maybe land a gig after college, too. Professor Williams would have no choice but to pick this, and Ashley could kiss my ass.*

As I toweled myself off, I ran the blow dryer through my hair, drying it just enough that my scalp wasn't dripping, but not completely drying it. I wanted to have loose waves.

On my way to class I was excited to start my rough draft of the interview. Nothing could bring me down today, not even Ashley.

I found my seat in the front of the classroom and jotted down my notes from a loose sheet of printer paper and filled up two pages. I wasn't sure if anyone but Ambrose would agree with this, but I crossed everything in hopes they'd all agree.

CJ had invited me to that day's practice and I knew that'd be my chance to ask, but I was afraid they'd all reject me.

I walked down the stairs, descending into Reginald's basement, a space I frequented when I wasn't lost in my studies. The small space had worn couches, a rug that was overdue for a shampooing and the glass for the studio was in need of a fresh coat of glass cleaner. I was shocked that everyone was still there ready to rock, except for Reg. "Where's Reg?"

"Still in the hospital, they're keeping him under observation."

"Wow, I'm sorry to hear that." I tried to sound as sincere as I could, but I knew this was a recurring thing for him. Ambrose vented to me a lot about his bandmates, but CJ was the one he rarely had anything bad to talk about. This also explains why I hadn't seen or heard from Pen.

Alexis stepped into the sound booth first as their friend Craig worked the mixing board. He was one of the best sound engineers in the underground business, as Ambrose told me several times.

"All right, Alexis. I want everything you've got. I need you to sing the shit out of this verse."

"Okay," she said, as she gathered her long dark hair into a low ponytail. She placed the headphones over her ears and grabbed the microphone with the tattered black glove that was covering her hand.

Goose bumps rose on my skin after hearing Alexis belt her heart out. I think this was going to be my new favorite song by Spasm.

They'd already had some of Reg's drum solos pre-recorded so they chopped and screwed it into the background as she sang. It had a nice, eclectic feel to it.

CJ went into the booth next and as he fingered his fret board, his eyes connected to mine, and I felt my heart speed up in my chest. He licked his thick, full lips and started singing along to parts of Alexis' pre-recorded lyrics.

I'm breaking down in pieces
Breaking down in pieces
Crack my shell
Tear my flesh away
The blood is gone,
But my heart is pained
Shattering bones
The Earth is my home
Fading from existence
But you found me
You gave me
A reason to believe
You found me
You gave me
The air I need to breathe

The look CJ had given me as our eyes connected through the glass was something unique. I felt like I'd inspired him, and motivated him to play the best damn guitar solo he could, and sing from some place deep down inside that he hadn't known existed.

I learned Reg might be in the hospital for a few more weeks and then was immediately going into rehab. It sucked, but it needed to be done. He has a problem, but CJ was convinced it wasn't his fault this time; he thinks those girls sabotaged him.

After their recording session, I gathered everyone on the couch and asked if I could interview them for my journalism project. I tried to talk them all up, inflated their egos, and that pretty much sealed the deal.

"Thank you so much, everyone! I'll interview you all one by one and maybe once Reg gets released, if there's time, I'll interview him too. You guys have no idea how much this means to me!"

Chapter 18

For the next few weeks everything that came out of Shannon's mouth was a fishing expedition for information. I thought this would be fun, but it was starting to piss me off. I felt like we weren't getting to know each other anymore, that I was just some words on paper. It started to get under my fucking skin.

"So, CJ, where are you from originally?"

"Shannon, can we not do this tonight? We can eat, fuck, drink, play Yahtzee—anything. I'm tired of all the damn questions. Besides, you already know where the hell I'm originally from."

She rolled her eyes and let out a huge sigh. "Sorry, I just want this to be good and as accurate as possible."

"It will be, but, damn, it's not like this is going into the *New York Times*. Can you take it down a notch?"

Clearly offended, she tossed her notebook back in her backpack, threw her pen at me and stormed out of my apartment. Normally I'd stop her, but I was happy as hell that she'd left—I needed to work on a new song, anyway.

After getting nowhere with these song lyrics, I called Alexis to ask for her opinion.

"Cody, I don't know how to put this—but—this song fucking sucks, dude. I can tell your head clearly isn't in it. What's going on?" Alexis asked, seeming genuinely concerned.

"I don't want to talk about it, but thanks for keeping it real with me."

"Go grab a drink, play with your cock for a while, and maybe the words will flow, all right? I'll see you tomorrow."

Laughing so hard my stomach hurt, I decided to do exactly what she said. Couldn't hurt, right?

Chapter 19

"Why did he have to be such a dick about it? He knows how much this article means to me!"

"Listen, Shan. As your best friend, I'm gonna have to agree with Cody. You've let this shit consume you and it's getting to the point where the lead guitarist of said band doesn't want to stick his dick in you right now, which you clearly need because you're so high strung. Ask Professor Dingleberry if he'll give you an extension and give it a rest. You're supposed to make Cody yours, not push him into the arms of a skank-ass groupie."

She was right. I was freaking out so much about this paper that I hadn't realized how big of a pain in the butt I was being. "Okay, I'll give it a rest. I'll email the professor in the morning and try to make amends with CJ before he hates me."

"Good girl."

I grabbed my laptop and scheduled an email to send Professor Williams in the morning.

It'd been a few days since I'd seen CJ and it hurt—a lot. I'd finally gotten him on the phone and he invited me to the band's practices again. I continued to interview the other bandmates, allowing him to come to me when he was ready to be questioned.

That night he invited me over to his apartment and I hoped he was finally ready to talk about things. Ruining whatever this was between us was stupid. Yes, my career was important, but having someone to share my career with was more rewarding. I didn't want to screw anything up. There was too much to be lost.

As I drove to Ambrose and CJ's apartment in my favorite skinny jeans and matching denim jacket, the butterflies in my stomach felt like they were just as confused as I was. I parked in front of his apartment complex and rubbed my hands against my legs as I climbed the stairs and rung the bell. *Here goes nothing!*

"Hey, make yourself at home; I need to grab a quick shower," he smirked, his eyes traveling up and down the length of my body, making me feel sexy but also a little insecure.

My brother had a typical bachelor pad. A small loveseat accompanied by a futon in the living room, the kitchen was sectioned off by a brick wall with a counter and table built in. My brother's bedroom was in the back of the living space, with the bathroom adjacent to it. And CJ's room was on the other side. It was way too small for me, but it worked for them.

I worked on my article until he came out of the shower— naked. He slid on a pair of basketball shorts and joined me on the couch. "Listen, Shan, I don't normally tell people about my past, but I feel I can trust you, so don't fuck this up, okay?"

"I won't, I promise."

"This is your one shot to ask me anything and I'll be honest to an extent that I can."

"Okay, before we start, where's my brother?"

"Don't worry. He's out for the night. I told him you were coming over to interview me and that he should chill elsewhere for the night."

"Okay, so where are you from originally?"

"British Columbia."

"You're Canadian? I always thought you were from here. I would have never guessed because you don't have an accent at all!"

"I don't, eh? Would this make you feel better, eh?" He

chuckled. "I was born there, but I didn't return until my thirteenth birthday."

"Shut up! I didn't mean it like that. I just meant, like, do you speak French or anything? And oh, so that's where you went!"

"Tu es très belle."

"What does that mean?"

"You are very beautiful." He ran his hand down the side of my cheek, gently tucking a strand of hair behind my ear. His subtle touch sent chills down my spine. "And trust me, it was not my choice to go back there. If I could have stayed here with you I would have."

I couldn't find the words to describe what I felt when I was around him. Trying to distract my brain from turning into goo, I started to ask him some more questions.

"When you were a kid, what did you want to be when you grew up?"

"A musician. Didn't my vintage t-shirts give that away?"

"They did! I still remember that shirt I bought for you."

"The Mötley Crüe one?"

"Yeah. I remember how much you loved it."

"I wore it until the seams burst, just so you know."

I couldn't help but grin from ear-to-ear. I'm glad my shirt stayed with him when I couldn't.

"So what made you want to become a musician?"

"Music has always been like therapy to me. I was never close to my dad, but my mom used to play it when we cleaned, played, and cooked. It just made me feel. It also had the power to help me forget."

"Forget what?"

"How much of a dick my father was to us and—"

"And?" The journalist in me wanted to question him further about his relationship with his father, but the part of me that really cared about him told me to stop because he'd tell me more about it when he was ready.

"You. It hurt for years, not knowing what to do. I was lost for a long time, Shannon."

"I was too, CJ." A hot tear slid from the corner of my eye and I quickly tried to change the subject. "How old are you?"

"You should know this, seeing as your brother is the same age as me, but I just turned twenty-four." He ran his hand over his chin, staring at me so hard I thought I had something in my teeth.

"What?"

"You really are beautiful, Shannon. You didn't have to doll yourself up just to come here and let me mess it all up." He leaned in and rubbed his nose against mine before our lips connected. This kiss was different. He kissed me hungrily, like he was trying to devour me, conquer me, and reclaim me.

He abruptly stopped, and it completely caught me off guard. "Continue with your interview, Shannon. I don't know how much longer I can keep my hands off of you."

Chapter 20

Shannon had interrogated me so thoroughly that I felt like the cops would burst through my door at any fucking minute. I wanted to fuck her so bad, and it was difficult to ignore how hot she looked sitting beside me. Her hair was pulled away from her face, and she had her glasses resting on her nose. The thin shirt she was wearing underneath her opened jacket revealed she was just as turned on as I was, but I had to wait. I wanted to get this shit over with so we could move on and not have to deal with another personal question ever again.

I don't know what made me do it, but I told her about some of my past. She had no idea the extent of trouble I was really in, and I didn't want to introduce her to it if I didn't have to.

Shannon had fallen asleep on the couch, so I put her laptop down and slid a sheet over her body. She curled up into a ball and never once opened her eyes. I sat back down on the couch, curious to see what she'd written about me. I knew I shouldn't have looked, but fuck, curiosity definitely killed the cat. *Only one line, Jamison.*

Title: Cody The Asshole?

That's enough for me.

"CJ, I'm so happy you agreed to do the interview, but off the record—I felt like you were holding back last night. You know I'd never hurt you right? You can trust me."

"I don't know who I can trust anymore, Shannon. I've been through a lot of shit."

"Okay, well I need to go and edit everything I have so far; if you want to talk more maybe you can come over after your show tonight?"

"Sure. See you then." Shannon grabbed her things and I immediately walked my ass back into the bathroom to handle this hard-on I'd had all fucking night.

It'd been a long time since I gave all my attention to one girl. Normally I'd fuck a different broad every night, sometimes two in the same night. I gave no fucks. But ever since I'd been hanging with Shannon, I hadn't wanted to hook up with anyone else, which was weird as hell because we weren't even together.

"I wasn't feeling that performance at all, guys, I'm going straight to the bar to drown my sorrows away. Anyone with me?" Alexis whined.

The show was dead as fuck tonight, but either way we got paid and instead of closing down the bar with the rest of Spasm, I had asked Kandy to give me a ride.

"You going back to your place tonight or hers?"

"Her who?"

"Shannon."

"Yeah, I'm going over there." After a quick stop, we pulled up in front of Shannon's place. "Thanks, Kand."

"Be good to this one, CJ. Ambrose would kill you if you hurt his baby sister."

"I know."

I hated to admit it, but Colt was a lucky fuck. Kandy was beautiful. Her brown hair stopped just at her shoulders, she never overdid it with the makeup, and her tits were utter perfection. She had a small quote tatted on her collarbone that read *live life fearlessly, welcome love effortlessly*. She kept most of our asses in line with her fiery Latina attitude.

I had picked up some Chinese food and a bottle of wine to set the mood because I couldn't go another night without being inside her. When I got to the door, Shannon seemed excited that I was there, but that's just how she was—*bubbly*.

"I'm so glad you're here! How was the show?"

"Fucking sucked. Let's eat."

Chapter 21

CJ seemed upset, and I didn't want to make things worse. After a few drinks and several empty Chinese food boxes, he practically vomited out the things he didn't have the heart to tell me the day before.

He admitted that the real reason he'd left town so abruptly was because his father got into some terrible gambling debts and had to flee the country and hide back in Canada. Since I'd assumed that debt was fulfilled, it struck me as odd when he mentioned he was still afraid of the mob.

"So is everything okay with your father now?"

"Not really. I'd been paying on his debt for the last five years. He got really sick and couldn't keep working for them."

"Okay, so why did you really come back here?"

"I wanted to make things right with you and Dean."

"Are you here legally?"

"No, but technically I never was. My parents forged my papers for school."

"Does anyone else know about this?"

"One person, the guy that helped me escape."

"What's his name?"

"I can't tell you that, Shan."

I don't know what possessed me to type all of this on my laptop, but it was good material. *It was the bottles of wine we drank*. It'd definitely get me to the top and Ashley could suck it. I knew it'd possibly hurt CJ if it got out, but seeing as only Professor Williams was going to read it, I didn't think CJ had to worry.

"Shannon."

"Yes?"

"Close the fucking laptop, get over here and place those pretty pink lips over my cock."

I hesitated for a moment too long and he closed it for me, pulling me over toward him and freed his cock from his pants. I licked my lips and did what he demanded. I was never one to take orders like this from others, but with him I liked it. I liked the dirty things he'd say to me, and the way he made my body feel.

CJ had crashed on my couch and I'd gone into my room and crashed there. I wanted us to sleep together, but he wouldn't wake up. I woke up in a panic the next day because I couldn't find my laptop. When I realized I'd left it on the couch and he was gone—I knew something was wrong.

I grabbed my phone and had one text from him.

> **CJ:** Fuck you, Shannon.

> **Me:** What did I do?

I'd had so much to drink the night before that I hadn't remembered what I'd done. I grabbed the laptop and turned it on. To my horror, I'd typed everything CJ told me in confidence. It wasn't a part of my article, but I'd opened a new document and added it there.

There was a note in the track changes that said *Really? After I let you in? Fuck you, Shannon, and if this gets out you'll pay for it.*

> **Me:** I'm sorry, CJ! I didn't mean to type everything! I never added it into the article and I'd never tell anyone what you told me!

> **CJ:** Go tell it to someone that fucking cares, lose my number you traitor.

"Oh my God, how could I have been so stupid? I'd never purposely hurt him, Pen. But now he hates me." I sobbed into her shoulder as she rested her hand on her stomach.

"Dude, you wrote a lot of fucked up things on here. Whether it was true or not, you fucked up. I don't think he'll ever forgive you for this. Were you drinking when you did this interview?"

"Yeah, I was. You know I can't filter myself well when I've been drinking. But I never meant to write down everything he said word for word." I noticed Pen wasn't touching the wine like she'd normally do when we were together. "Are you all right, Pen?"

"Yeah, why?"

"You're not drinking."

"I think you'll require this whole bottle tonight, love. I'll just grab some water. I haven't been feeling well lately. I think I have a stomach bug or something."

She was lying to me, I could tell by the look on her face. She'd been sick for at least a month now. I took the entire bottle and placed it up to my lips, tilting my head back and letting the sweet bubbly liquid slide down my throat, numbing the pain I felt in my heart.

I'd called, texted, and emailed CJ, but he wouldn't respond to me. *Dammit, Shannon. You just got him back and now you've ruined things.*

Chapter 22

Two months later

"Harder, harder, harder. Don't you know how to suck a cock properly? Christ."

I felt like this had to be a fucking joke. Every night this week I've had some broad promise me a good time, and then fail miserably at it. Was this what my life was being reduced to? Being let down by a girl that looked like Barbie, but sucked cock like a dying fish out of water? Or was it all karma for thinking I could be honest with someone and them throw it all back in my fucking face?

I'd been spiraling out of control ever since the fallout with Shannon a couple months back. I didn't want to see her or talk to her, and as much as it hurt, it had to be done. She betrayed me. She was the last person I thought would hurt me. All my life my father had manipulated and used me, but I never expected the woman I loved to do it, too. At least not this one.

My current failure was named Christy, or was it Brenda? Shit, I don't know. Whatever her name was, I wanted her to go away, which was a shame because she was so hot. Big luscious tits, long blonde hair, and beautifully tanned legs that went on for miles. She wore a skintight leather dress and there was no panty line in sight. At first glance, she looked like she meant business, but boy was I wrong.

"I'm sorry, Mr. Jamison. I'm just really nervous," she said

gazing up at me from her knees on the bathroom floor, before wrapping her lips back around my length.

That's better. Maybe there's hope for this one after all.

The plus side of being in a band was the endless pussy that was thrown your way. After our second show, another groupie followed me into the bathroom. This one came prepared. She led me into the largest stall, and lifted her very tiny skirt, exposing her bare ass. She rubbed it up against me, then turned around and unfastened my belt and went to town on my cock. It didn't take much for him to get aroused, and I had to stop her before I released my load all over her face. If her mouth felt this good, I knew her pussy had to feel even better. I yanked a handful of her dark hair and brought her back to her feet, gently running my tongue down the side of her neck. I spun her around and made her lift one leg and rest her foot on the toilet. She surpassed my expectations when she placed her foot on the metal bar beside it.

Her pink flesh was completely exposed and my cock ached as I slid the latex down my shaft. I guided my head toward her entrance and gently pierced her folds. "Take me, Cody. I want to feel you deep inside of me."

I never gave a girl what she wanted, when she wanted. I learned pretty quickly that they'll betray you at the first opportunity. I liked things to be on my terms and this girl was going to learn. I'd torture her until she begged me to give her a release.

I pulled out and then rubbed my head against her clit, while she bucked against me, trying to slide back on it, but I wouldn't let her. "What's wrong, sweetheart?" I growled in her ear.

"Please make me feel good."

"Why should I?"

Before she had the chance to speak, I dipped a finger inside of her, curling my fingers against her insides, torturing her. Her body tensed around my fingers and I knew I had her just where I wanted her.

I replaced my fingers with my cock and fucked her until she was screaming my name. Just as I was about to release, Randy, the security guard, knocked on the door. He always knocked three times when things got a little too loud. Nearing my release, I slammed into her a few more times, and as she tightened around me, we both moaned in ecstasy.

I tossed the condom in the trash and went to go wash my hands. I left the stall opened and noticed the girl had sat down on the toilet. "You all right?"

"Yeah, just sore."

"Good. Well, thanks for that. I have another show to get ready for."

"Can I give you my number?"

Not again. I swear they never learn. It's just a one and done deal with me. No strings and no commitment. I hated this part. This was where I'd be known as the royal asshole.

"Listen D—"

"It's Marie."

"Marie, I'm not really looking for anything serious right now. I'm sure you expected that, right?"

"No. I thought you might be different. It's not like you're actually a huge rock star." *Ouch.*

"I'm not a rock star yet, but I will make your panties wet. Oh wait, been there and done that. Nice try, toots."

"You're such an asshole, Cody."

"That's Jamison to you," I said as I walked through the steel door. Randy was standing at the end of the hallway, smiling at me.

"Another one bites the dust, huh, CJ?"

"You know it. I don't know why this is so hard for them to grasp." Randy was your typical bouncer. Big, bald, with a neatly trimmed goatee, and was covered in tattoos.

"Maybe it's the way your ass looks in those leather pants."

I cupped my left ass cheek in my hand. "I guess so." We both laughed loudly. Little miss sunshine finally came out of the bathroom and gave me the middle finger as she walked by. I placed a hand over my heart, pretending to be hurt, then laughed and grabbed my junk.

"Asshole!"

"You weren't saying that when you were coming on my dick a few minutes ago."

"Ugh!" She huffed, storming out of the back exit, bumping into Dean as he entered.

"Hey, CJ," he said with a smirk on his face.

"Sup, idol?" We nicknamed Dean "The Idol" because we all respected him. And he definitely looked like a legendary rocker, with the long dark hair on the top of his head, shaved sides, the music notes on his chest that spread around his arm. He towered over all of us. When he spoke, his deep voice commanded your full attention.

"Nothing much. You ready for later? I heard a few scouts from Periscope Records will be at the Paradise Isle event. My boy Thomas told me that they've listened to a few of our songs on YouTube and were interested in seeing us live. They want to make sure we're legit."

"No shit? This isn't gonna be a fluke like that shit with ACD Records, right?"

"No shit. But judging by the disappointment on that girl's face, I'd suggest you keep it in your pants until after our performance. And nah, this is nothing like that."

"You're such a dick. See you later."

"Oh and Reg is back tonight, so try not to mention the 'rehab' word."

"I won't."

Periscope Records was a big fucking deal. They had the power to skyrocket your career and I was ready for it. I'd been in trouble my entire life, always running away from my problems and never really wanting to do much with myself. Music was always my way to cope when things were getting really shitty. I had become very cautious with these labels and deals because ACD was trying to change everything about us and take a 70/30 split of our royalties.

Things were finally starting to pick up and being on the road would help me forget—forget about her. *And our boy was finally back.*

"All right, germs and germettes, are you ready to hear some real fucking rock n' roll?" Alexis shouted to the crowd in front of us. Her long dark hair with the bright red streaks was illuminated by the spotlights beaming directly on her.

Reg tapped his sticks together, initiating a three count and I made love to my guitar strings with my fingers as the rest of the band slowly joined the sequence one by one. He'd been gone for a while after that night and we were so fucking glad to have him back. We'd had a stand-in, his cousin Joe, and Joe was good, but Reg was the fucking man.

"I love you, CJ!" I heard someone yell from the crowd before a pair of lace panties flew onto the stage landing at my feet. Girls were getting out of control the more shows we did, but it amped me up even more. I lived for the attention.

As Alexis sang her harmony, chills went up my spine. This was a song I'd written in a pinch. It was titled "The Fire in your Eyes."

> *The way you look at me, with the fire in your eyes, burns into my soul*
>
> *Scarring me deep down, so deep I can feel my insides bleeding*
>
> *But don't cry for me; heal me with your loving arms*
>
> *Don't hate me for the person I used to be, help me become a better me*

I could see tears form in every single girls' eyes in the crowd. *Jackpot.*

"Thank you!" we all said in unison as we took our exit from the stage.

"You guys were phenomenal!" said a tall man wearing dark shades, as we approached the hallway to head back to our dressing room.

"Thanks, man. And you are?"

"Sebastian Arnold."

"Wait. *The* Sebastian Arnold?" Alexis squealed.

"Yes. I love your band's sound. You guys have a unique quality and I'd love to hear more of your live work."

I thought Alexis was going to faint right in front of him. As he walked closer to us, I could see he had rings on each of his fingers. He handed his card to Dean.

"When's your next show?"

"Tomorrow at the Agave Theater."

"I will be there. You guys have really impressed me tonight, but you need to *wow* me tomorrow." Sebastian was a mysterious man. He was taller than me, with a bald head and wore an all black suit. He disappeared from our group and we headed back to our dressing room, each of us with a huge smile on our faces. *This is it, I can feel it.*

Chapter 23

I'd been up all night working on some new material for the band to play. Something about talking to Sebastian really motivated me. I really wanted to make a statement at the Agave Theater.

"What ya workin' on, CJ?" Alexis asked. She looked sexy as hell today, and it pained me that she was completely off limits. When she wore that sexy red lipstick it made her look extra fuckable, but she made it clear she was only into girls. Occasionally her girlfriend, Mel, kept her company after a show.

"Just another song."

"Oh, yeah? Can I read it?"

"Of course. You know I always need to hear you sing it to know if it's legit."

She smiled at me as I handed her my notebook. I stared at her breasts as she sat down on the couch. "Coursing through my veins? I like it already!"

> *I can feel the darkness surrounding me – swallowing me whole*
> *The leather ring around my arm is dragging me down*
> *The fire coursing through my veins makes me feel alive*
> *The comfort that it's giving me can never be undone*
> *But why is it so hard?*

I cut myself so deep
I put myself to sleep — eternally
The blood stains on the carpet, reminding her of what I
used to be
A trail of lies that drained her soul, remaining by my side
It was so hard to breathe
The lies you believed
You cried yourself to sleep — protecting me
But I can't tell you how much you mean to me — anymore
But, I love you

"Dude—that is fucking deep. Where did this come from?"

"My cousin Aaron died of an overdose years ago and I just thought of him, and boom."

"Well, shit, we need to practice this as soon as possible. It'll be perfect for the performance at the Agave! I'll go get the guys."

In a matter of hours, we had the melody, hook and everything down pat. I couldn't believe these guys trusted me to write lyrics that we'd actually performed, let alone ones I'd just written. But we were all a team and we knew our time to shine was coming.

We were on our way to the theater and my stomach started to roll. I was so nervous to perform this brand new tune in front of a bunch of strangers and potential scouts. I knew we had what it took, but I'm not afraid to admit I was a little scared.

"Hey, CJ. You all right man?" Dean asked.

"Yeah, you know how I get about my songs."

"Dude, it's fucking amazing. If this song doesn't wow Sebastian, then he's on fucking crack."

Colt started the soft melody on the keyboard and I joined in on lead guitar before Alexis started the first line. She had so much power and soul in her raspy voice. She had the ability to make you feel every single lyric. Her voice was our secret weapon.

Hearing my words and singing along with four of my best friends was the best feeling in the world. Once the song finished, we had a standing ovation. That had never happened to us before and I think we were all taken aback by it. Shit, I know I was.

The crowd chanted for an encore, but we had to get off the stage to let the next band perform in their allotted time frame. *I can't wait for the day we have the stage to ourselves.*

As we exited the stage, every single person that worked behind the scenes gave us a round of applause, including Sebastian.

"Okay, which one of you wrote that song? It was powerful as hell and I want to hear more just like it."

Dean pushed me forward. "Here's your guy."

"You wrote that? I wouldn't have pegged you for a writer."

What the fuck is that supposed to mean?

"Have you ever considered becoming a professional songwriter for others?"

I choked on air hearing him say that. "I don't think I'm ready for that. I'm good with writing songs for our band. This is where my heart is. Thank you, though."

"Well, if you ever want to venture into the world of songwriting the offer is still on the table, but for now, I'd love to see you all in my office at Periscope Records at ten o'clock tomorrow morning."

"What? Are you serious?" Alexis shouted, jumping up and down so much her breasts almost spilled out of her tight, low cut top.

"As a heart attack, my dear. I'd love to hear another new song by then. It's okay if it's not finished, I just want to see how well you work under pressure."

"You got it!"

"You've got a long night ahead of you, Cody."

"What do you mean, Dean?"

"You have less than twenty-four hours to write us another partial hit."

Shit. Like I needed any added pressure.

"Alexis! Wake up!"

Everyone had crashed in the recording studio, except me. It was really early in the morning, but I was finally able to come up with a few bars of a new song to present to Sebastian that day.

"What? I'm up. You better have a fucking hit or I'll slice one of your nuts off!"

"It'd be worth it, if you touched them. But all bullshit aside, read this!"

"Powerless."
Powerless, I feel powerless
You took control of everything
My mind
My soul
My heart's grown cold
I will never feel alone
Powerless, you left me powerless
I feel trapped behind your walls
You've sucked me dry; no more tears to cry
My pride has finally died

"Dude this would make a killer ballad. I think you're secretly a chick on the inside."

"Or I've been in so many chicks, their girlishness rubbed off on me."

She elbowed me. "You're such a pig, but that's why I love you!"

"Love you, too. I'll write another one, just in case."

"Good. I want to sing something that'll bring the fuckin' house down!"

"Go get some sleep. We have to be there in about," I paused to look at my cell, "five hours. That'll give me plenty of time to come up with a few bars of something new."

"Good. It's your turn to get coffee this time. Make sure you get mine black with extra sugar!"

"Of course."

Time to get to work.

Battered and Bruised

The fresh marks on your skin are for his pleasure and your pain

The long sleeves, the makeup are for his personal gain

I watch from the distance, hurting from your hell

Wanting to pound my knuckles right across his skull

You begged me – no

You pleaded – no

I see what you're worth

You're more than a skirt

I'm saving you from his torture

Black and blue doesn't suit you

Let me repay you by healing you

Damaged goods

You're not damaged goods

You're a princess, a damsel that needs to be saved

A princess, and no longer his slave

You're no longer his slave

We arrived in front of this huge, round, thirty-story building with a large needle at the top. I'd never seen a building like this before in my life. Each floor was surrounded by small, square, tinted windows, and I couldn't imagine the magic that had been produced behind each one. My heart sped up so fast that I thought I'd pass out before we stepped through the doors.

Once we mustered the balls to walk through the huge glass entryway, we were greeted by the receptionist, Janice. She gave us a pass to head on up. She told us that she was expecting us and wished us luck. Sebastian's office was on the twentieth floor and waiting for the elevator to come back to ground level was agonizing.

As the doors to the elevator opened, the lead singer of Metrix, Johnny Starr, walked off. He looked at us and my inner fangirl came out. "Hey, you guys here for an audition?"

"Yeah," I said, trying to choke back a scream. He extended his hand toward mine and the eyeball tattoo on his hand looked even cooler up close.

He reminded me of a skinnier version of Dean, only his voice wasn't as deep. "That's cool. What's your names?"

Since everyone else was too star-struck to speak, I introduced everyone. "This is Ambrose, Colt, Reg, Alexis, and I'm Cody. Our band is Spasm."

"Nice to meet you all. Well, y'all have the look down, hopefully you've got the talent to back it up. See you around and good luck!"

We stepped inside the elevator and as soon as the door shut, Alexis jumped up and down squealing like a damn banshee. "O.M.G he's like the only guy who could possibly turn me straight."

"I could turn you straight too, Red."

"Eh, unlikely. You can still be my best friend, though."

"Oh, friend-zoned." I grabbed at my chest, and squeezed my eyes shut, dropping my head in playful shame.

We'd finally reached the twentieth floor and I swear the entire atmosphere changed once the doors opened. Everything seemed to move in super slow motion. We were greeted by a hot little number named Tess, and if I weren't with the band, I'd have planned to bend her over a desk and fuck her until her tits popped out of her top. She had fire-engine red hair, tattoos were peeking out from underneath her long sleeves and I could tell by the look in her eyes, she'd be nothing but a good time. "Mr. Arnold will see you now."

We walked into this huge office, with windows stretched from the ceiling to the floor. There was a huge-ass leather sectional that could sit about twenty people, and his desk was in the back of the room with a shit-ton of plaques and records covering the wall. He also had a small recording studio in the far wing of this suite and he was sitting in front of the sound mixer with a huge black guy accompanying him. "Hope you guys are ready. This here is Tyrone and he's the best sound mixer in the business. If he can't make you guys sound authentic, then no one can."

The knots in my stomach tightened, but I quickly got my shit together. I'd been waiting for this moment for what seemed like my whole life and not a damn person was going to ruin my shot. Sebastian opened the door to the sound booth and we all went inside. The instruments inside were brand new and I couldn't wait to make love to the black and red Fender. Another sexy assistant came in and hooked us all up with headphones and made sure all of our microphones worked. *I can't wait to land this gig. There is nothing but hot, untapped ass in here that I'd love to hit.*

Alexis looked at each one of us to make sure we were ready to rock and we all gave her a middle finger, letting her know we were good to fucking go.

After our first session, Sebastian stood up and gave us a stern look scaring the complete shit out of me, because he was very hard to read. *Did he like it? Did he hate it? Would he tell us to get the fuck out of his studio and never return?* He surprised us when he asked us to continue and play another song. Not too many people have scared me in my life, but he was definitely one intimidating motherfucker.

We played our hearts out and performed two more songs for him before he told us to take a break for lunch and he'd have our answer when we returned.

There was a diner on the corner named Jim's Best Barbecue and we all found a booth in the back. "Dude, that was scary as fuck," Colton said, quickly chugging back a cup of water.

"I know, but I think we nailed it. Why else would he let us perform all three songs, unless he was interested in at least one?"

"I'm so nervous, I can't even eat. I think I'll just grab a milkshake," Alexis interrupted.

After our quick lunch, we returned to Sebastian's office, my legs were shaking as he told us all to have a seat on the couch.

"So how'd you like Jim's?"

"It was delicious!" Alexis answered.

"Great. Now let's get to business. You guys sound amazing. I think with a little more fine-tuning, you guys could take the world by storm. I'd love to be your manager and offer you a six-month contract with Periscope Records. You'll have the option to extend it once we feel things out and see if we're a good match together. Or we can part ways."

I felt like I was dreaming. He didn't just offer us a six-month contract? Right? This is a joke. It has got to be a fucking joke.

"Mr. Arno—"

"Call me Sebastian."

"Sebastian, I don't even know what to fucking say right now. You've made my entire year," Reg said, tapping his legs with some pens he'd found on the table.

"I'll have my assistant, Tess, come in and draw up the paperwork. Would you guys still like to be called Spasm?"

"Yes, the name is not up for negotiation, Sebastian—ever," Dean quickly responded.

"Good, I wouldn't have it any other way."

Chapter 24

It'd been two months since I'd seen CJ or any of the other band members of Spasm. Even my own brother had been kind of distant lately and it sucked so badly. Ever since they'd met with a few scouts, they'd been in the studio non-stop trying to get their demo together.

Pen had been sick constantly, and although she couldn't keep much down, her face was rounding out. She still wouldn't tell me what was wrong, but I knew she was pregnant, a few months along by now.

I looked down at my phone and saw a picture I'd saved of CJ, immediately feeling an ache in my heart. Before school break, I'd decided to ask the Professor for an extension on my article, because my head wasn't in it. All I could think about was CJ and how I could get him back. When I lost him before it was out of my control, but this time it was my doing.

> **Me:** Pen, do you know where the band is traveling to tonight?
>
> **Pen:** They'll be staying at the Ultra Hotel and performing at the Five Below Club.
>
> **Me:** Thank you.
>
> **Pen:** Do u need me for backup?
>
> **Me:** No, I got this. I ruined this and I have to be the one to fix it.

Pen: *Go get him, tiger! The show starts at eight!*

You can do this, Shannon. You can get him to forgive you.

I yanked the sexiest red dress I had out of my closet and slid it over my lingerie set. This dress made my breasts look spectacular and the material hugged every curve of my body. If wearing this couldn't get him to forgive me then I don't know what would.

I admired myself in my floor-length mirror, coating my lips with a shade of dark lipstick and giving my curls a quick fluff before I grabbed my purse, slid on my long trench coat and got into my car.

The hotel was a thirty-minute drive from my apartment and that gave me plenty of time to come up with absolutely no strategy. I pulled up in front of the luxurious hotel and the valet greeted me at my door. After staring at me so hard I thought he was going to eat me, I handed him my keys and he assured me that he'd take care of my baby for me.

The doorman held the glass door open and smiled at me as I walked into the enormous lobby. The walls were coated in gold and white intricate designs and a crystal chandelier was molded into the ceiling, with spare lines of crystals hanging a few inches from the floor over a small pool of water. I'd never seen anything that extravagant in my life.

I approached the check-in desk, and if I hadn't worn heels I wouldn't have been able to see over the top of it. "How may I help you, miss?"

"I was wondering if I could get a room for the night."

"Our rate for a standard room is two hundred and fifty dollars, plus tax."

"Are you serious?"

"Yes, very."

Think Shannon.

"Come closer." The clerk, a young blond, handsome thing bent down and I pressed my lips as close to his ear as I could without actually making contact.

"There's nothing you could do?"

"No, I'm sorry. I'd lose my job."

"A little birdy told me that the band Spasm was staying here. My older brother, Ambrose, just so happens to be a part of the band."

"Oh, well, why didn't you say so? I can't give you a discount, but your brother may be able to get you a room in their block. Here's the room he's in," he said, slipping me a piece of paper with a room number and the floor they were on. "Make sure you come back with him or his manager."

"Thank you."

As I approached the tenth floor, I felt the bile rise in my stomach. The inside of the elevator was a reflective gold, and looking at myself in it, I immediately became self-conscious. I felt like a prostitute, but if this is what it took, then so be it.

The bell rang and the doors split. Alexis was in the hallway talking to another female and I tried to sneak by without being noticed. "Shannon? Is that you? You look amazing."

Busted. "Thanks, have you seen—"

"CJ? Yeah, he's downstairs, but take this." She slid a keycard into my hand. "Our rooms are connected, so you can sneak in through mine. I won't be in it tonight." She looked back at the gorgeous female in front of her and smiled.

"Thank you!"

A sense of relief washed over me as I searched for Alexis's room. I slid the key in the handle and felt like my breath had left my body. It must really pay to be an up-and-coming rock star.

I scanned the room and I couldn't help but admire everything in it. It was huge. A large window stretched the entire length of the room with a view of the water. There was a large flat screen mounted to the wall with an electric fireplace underneath. The bed was big enough to fit four people comfortably and the white linen looked so fluffy and soft that I wanted to pounce on it and let the softness take me away. The warm beige walls gave the room a very welcoming feel.

I ran my hand over the velvet curtain and looked out at the water.

My phone buzzed in my purse and I had a feeling who it might be, but I was shocked at the face that scrolled across my screen. *Ambrose.*

"H-hello?"

"Hey, I just wanted to see how you were."

"I'm okay. And you?"

"Okay, listen, I have a show tonight, and I'd really like to see you there."

"I'll be there."

"I'm gonna assume you already know where to go?"

"Yeah, Penelope told me."

"Cool, see you then."

I unlocked the door that joined the two rooms and snuck a peek into CJ's room. It was identical to Alexis's, but somehow had a more masculine feel. I heard his doorknob rattle and quickly shut the door. *Crap, that was a close one.*

Chapter 25

"Spasm! Spasm! Spasm!" Could this be real life? Thousands of fans chanting, no, *screaming* for us, as we stood behind the black curtain. Adrenaline was flooding my veins as I jumped up and down to calm myself down.

"Y'all ready for this shit?" Reg questioned, twirling his sticks around his fingers.

"As ready as we'll ever be!" Alexis answered.

"Now let's welcome to the stage, the band you've all been waiting for—Spasm!"

The curtain was pulled back and hot, blinding lights flashed in my eyes as we ran to take our positions on the stage. The smoke from the fog machines was thick, and when Red grabbed her microphone, the lights dimmed to a cool shade of blue as she seduced the crowd with her words. "Since you already know who the hell we are, let's get this shit started!"

Chasing the light
Running free, I'm running far
Bright lights ahead, spacing through cars
The rain on my skin, runs fast, feels cold
It's washing me, cleansing my soul
A piece of me left in this space, running from you
A complete disgrace

But I'm out of time, I've run too far
Gaining more speed, I've gone too far
It's in my head, I've done my deed
Nothing inside me feels complete
But the light is near, the dark is far, chasing the light, it
feels so small
Deep in my bones, I've felt this place
The light is home, my safe escape
The light shines bright, the light feels right
Chasing the light
Chasing the light
Shines so bright
Shines so bright
Deep in my bones, I've felt this place
The light is home, my safe escape
Two minutes
Two minutes since you left me
Two minutes you've been gone
Two minutes since the blow ensued
Two minutes since I've thought of you
Every minute, every hour
Watching the clock, I cower
On the floor in the shower I think of you
Oo-oo-oo
I think of you
Oo-oo-oo
The look on your face, can't be replaced
You took your life, a big mistake
Nothing feels good, we're both dead now
But I'm alive, you're underground
I'm missing you

Oo-oo-oo

I'm missing you

Oo-oo-oo

You've got to kiss me in the dark

The dark, the dark

Your touch it's tearing me apart

Apart, apart

You'll never see me in the day

The day, the day

Because he will not go away

Away, away

Completely defeated, my life's not completed

Without him, I'm needed by you

The force was so strong, so very wrong

The band on my hand

A discreet misunderstanding

From the man, my heart no longer wants

What I want is you, what I need is true

But I can't give myself to you

So will you kiss me in the dark?

The dark, the dark

Your touch it's tearing me apart

Apart, apart

You'll never see me in the day,

The day, the day

Because a secret this must stay

Must stay, must stay

You'll never understand

How much I want you as my man

My man, my man

But the ring on my hand, binds me to the wrong one

I hope you understand — he'll never be like you
He'll never be like you

After a killer performance like that, I'd usually be down to fuck a hot broad that night, but I couldn't. *What the fuck is wrong with me?* I was whipped by a girl, who I confided in and she wanted to use that shit against me. Hopefully the alcohol in my mini-fridge would make all these conflicting *feelings* fuck off.

"CJ, aren't you gonna hit the bar with us tonight?"

"Nah, I'm good. I'll see y'all later, Colt."

I quickly slipped away from the band and fought through a shit-ton of groupies to make it in the elevator—alone. *Fuck.*

I approached the tenth floor, stuck my head out the door, making sure the coast was clear before I went to my room. I pulled my key out of my pocket after looking over my shoulder for the millionth time, and slid the keycard in. The red light flashed green, and I immediately noticed that the light was on in my room.

"Hello? Who's in here?" I yelled as I rounded the corner. I found Shannon sitting on my bed, a few empty bottles decorated the floor in front of her, and she had my spare guitar straddled between her legs. "Shannon, what are you doing here?" She wouldn't answer me. "What the fuck do you want, Shannon? Huh? Are you here to confuse the hell out of me some more? Are you here to dangle yourself in front of me like a piece of steak in front of a hungry wolf? You can't break in here and act like everything is fine after that bullshit you pulled."

"CJ, I'm sorry. I never wanted things to be like this."

"Well they are and you fucked up. Never in my life have I opened up to someone like I did with you, and all you did was spit in my face. But yet, I'm the asshole because I'm moving on and going for my dreams. You're the only one who knows about my past. Did that even fucking matter to you?"

Her eyes darted to the ground, and her arms crossed her chest as if she were trying to keep herself warm. "CJ, it matters,

I just didn't realize what I was doing."

"Obviously. Now that I'm fucking other girls, you want to come back. Why do you care now? I haven't heard from you in months. No apology, nothing, fucking nada! How'd the article come out? Did you get an A for fucking effort?"

"I never turned the project in, CJ. And if I'm not mistaken, you're the one who wouldn't return any of my phone calls. I had to be sure I knew what I wanted. Haven't you ever questioned things? Hasn't your heart ever wanted something that your brain told you you shouldn't have?"

"Yes. And that's you. I was willing to commit myself to one girl. The things I felt for you were unreal and I knew I wouldn't be able to hold my shit together without you and I can't."

"I can still be that, CJ."

"I can't fucking trust you anymore, Shannon. How do I know you're not here to gather more material for another article? I don't, so please just go."

Chapter 26

I'd done it. I'd broken Cody Jamison. I knew since the first time that I saw him that he was special. I'd been able to unlock something from deep within him that was only for me. That shine, that luster, and now it's gone. And I don't think I'll ever get it back.

He ran his hands through his hair, his brown eyes full of hurt and it twisted my insides knowing that I did this to him. I caused him this unnecessary pain. And for what? Because I was a coward, a scared little girl that let her potential dream job hurt the person I've loved since I was nine years old.

I stepped forward, reaching for his hand, but he pushed it away. "Don't. You don't get to fucking touch me anymore."

I felt hot tears building in the corners of my eyes, the water sliding down my cheeks, searing my soul. *What have I done?*

That night I sat alone in my apartment, ignoring Penelope's constant calls, texts, and random drop-bys. I needed to be by myself, I needed to suffer for what I'd done to him. *CJ.*

Thinking about him made my heart ache; remembering the way he looked at me made my soul hurt—I was dead inside.

Sitting in this dark space made everything feel so small. The four walls surrounding me felt as if they were closing in. I had to escape. I had to go find him, make him talk to me. I didn't do depressed—not anymore.

I tossed my winter jacket over my shoulders, and slipped my feet inside my fuzzy winter boots, leaving my wallet and phone behind. I grabbed my keys off the stand and as I opened the door, the wind was immediately knocked out of me.

CJ . . .

"What are you doing here?" His back was toward me, but the smell of alcohol was hanging in the air.

"I had to see you. I had to make things right."

"I was on my way back to the hotel; I couldn't handle the guilt anymore. You were the last person I ever wanted to hurt and I realized that I love you, CJ. I always have and always will. I'm yours forever—if you'll have me."

Chapter 27

That night I realized how much of a douche I was being, courtesy of Alexis. I'd told her everything that happened between Shannon and me, excluding the whole mob thing. Once she told me how Shannon got into my room and smacked me upside my head a few times, I realized I could have at least given her a chance. The girl was piss drunk, on my bed in a sexy-ass dress, and I whined about my feelings.

I didn't normally chase chicks, but this was different. Yes, Alexis was on my ass, but I couldn't say what really pushed me over the edge. Maybe it was stupidity? Lust? Love? Alcohol? Whatever it was, I hated how it felt. I hated not having her. I hailed the first cab I could to her apartment. I tried calling her cell, but she wouldn't answer. I knocked on the door several times, and no answer. I couldn't blame her for not wanting to talk to me after the selfish asshole I'd become. I didn't even give her a chance to say anything.

I felt like an idiot sitting on her steps, but I didn't want to leave. Just in case she wasn't home, I wanted to be there waiting for her, to apologize. I wanted to be there to give her the comfort she deserved.

It was cold and windy as fuck. The breeze pushed the snow around, making it dance in the air as it hit me in the face. *Ouch.*

I heard keys rattle against the door and it opened. I turned around and she jumped back. "What are you doing here?"

"I had to see you. I had to make things right."

"I'm so sorry."

"No, Shannon—I'm sorry."

I got up off the steps and brushed the remaining snowflakes off my clothes. She looked so beautiful—even with her tear-stained cheeks and bloodshot eyes.

Her brown hair was in a messy clump on the top of her head, and she had these glorified snow boots on that looked like my nana's old house slippers. Her lip curled up into a half-smile and I knew she was mine again. I pushed my way through her door, slamming it shut behind me, feeling the heat from her body against my own. I placed my hand behind her neck, my lips hovering mere centimeters away from hers. "You hold the power, Shan. Tell me to leave and I will. But if not, I'm going to take you into that back room, and reclaim what's always been mine."

Silence has never sounded so good.

I stepped out of my boxers and tossed them atop the huge pile of clothes beside me, admiring every curve of her body from the edge of the bed. Her freckles were like mini chocolate morsels covering her thighs. I couldn't wait to run my tongue across them. I needed to appreciate every part of her tonight, because there was nothing else I wanted—or needed—more than Shannon Moore. Without her, the music was nothing. Without her, I didn't feel whole. Without her, my well had gone dry.

Inhale.

Exhale.

Take back what's mine.

"Touch yourself."

"What would you like me to touch?" she whispered roughly, clearly just as turned on as I was.

"Your breasts."

She ran her hands over her bare tits, carefully and sensually caressing each once with her hand. Twisting her stiff buds, and moaning as she switched sides. I pumped my cock in my hand, watching her, stalking her, waiting.

Without saying another word, her hands traveled further south, spreading her lips apart and rubbing in between. *Fuck, that's hot.*

"Shannon, please tell me you got on birth control. I need to feel you, all of you, raw and unrestricted."

"Yes," she breathed heavily, almost coming undone by her own touch. "I got the implant in my arm, I'm safe for th-three years."

Good girl.

Her lip retracted between her teeth when she was close to orgasm. I watched, spellbound, as she rubbed her bud faster, until I interrupted. "Not so fast—save some for me." I grabbed her hand and stuck her fingers in my mouth, sucking her essence off them. *Fuck.*

"Open your eyes Shannon," I growled as I rubbed my cock against her thigh. "I want you to look at me."

She blinked rapidly as I slid my raw length inside of her tight opening. And as if on cue, her eyes pinched together. "Open them."

Chapter 28

Lying on my back, pleasuring myself in front of CJ, was exhilarating. I'd never done anything like that ever in my life, and I craved more. I'd barely touched myself at all until he came back into my life, and it was like I couldn't get enough. The thought of him, the smell of him, the intense desire that laced his eyes—his touch—it was my drug.

He growled at me, demanding that I keep my eyes opened; he wanted to make me see everything. I tried to, but as soon as he slid inside of me, raw, unrestricted, and real—my eyes shut. "Open them, Shannon."

I opened them and what I saw looking back at me was different. He held himself on top of me, we were connected as one, and he was staring into my eyes. His heart was speaking to mine, and mine was speaking to his. He ran his hand down the side of my face, tucking a stray strand of hair behind my ear, and then kissed me.

His tongue traveled under my chin and down the crease of my breasts, but we still remained connected. He pulled a nipple into his mouth and pumped, then pulled the other into his mouth and pumped again. Teasing me, torturing me, making me want to scream in anticipation.

"You're forgiven, Shannon," he said as the dark luster in his eyes returned. He rocked my hips slowly, stretching me, pulling one leg up over his shoulder and kissing my ankle before grabbing it and pounding into me. I was warm all over. I could feel the orgasm building, rippling through my core, my mound clutching his cock as the warmth from within him shot inside of me, but he didn't stop. He slammed into me, like an animal, my hands reaching behind him, my nails clawing into his firm flesh. I'd lost total control. My body seized so much, I'd forgotten where I was. The tingling sensation that remained after he broke our bond and wrapped his arms around me was pure bliss.

I awoke to the smell of actual food being cooked in my apartment. I'd gotten so lazy that I barely ever cooked. I ordered out for the majority of my meals, or had some dinners in the freezer. CJ was like a pure animal the night before, we'd had so much sex I didn't think I was able to orgasm anymore, but he certainly proved me wrong every time. I don't know how the hell he could have a sex-a-thon and get up and cook me breakfast. Maybe he was a freak of nature.

CJ poked his head through the opened door and smiled at me. He made a makeshift tray out of old cardboard boxes to put over my lap with a platter full of waffles, strawberries, and bacon. "I wasn't sure if you liked eggs, but I do have some of those too."

"I'm not a big egg fan, but thank you. This smells delicious. Wait, where did you get these? And when did you have the time to go and get it?"

"You ask too many questions, just eat, Shannon."

I cut into the waffle, took a swipe of the butter and spread it across the top before taking a bite. "Oh my God, this tastes just like—"

"Your mom's? She'd passed the recipe over to my mom and I made sure I learned how to perfect it, so that one day if I were able to, I could make them for you. I hope I've done it justice."

The waffles practically melted in my mouth, and I couldn't get over the gesture he'd made. I'd missed these so much, and every bite took me back to my youth. "CJ, I just—thank you. You've done it more than justice; I think these might even be better. Don't tell my mom, though."

He smirked. "Your secret is safe with me, hon. What happened to your parents anyway?"

"They moved to Florida a few years back. Dad's computer company relocated and Mom was able to start her own event planning business. I talk to them on the phone sometimes, but I haven't seen them in a long time."

"I see."

"Mom was so happy when I told her you came back."

"Yeah?"

"She always liked you, CJ."

"I always liked her, too."

Chapter 29

Cody

"You're in a chipper mood today. Did you finally get some?" Alexis winked at me. The guys all looked at me with their eyebrows pinched together, confused, but I wasn't telling them shit. We had to get this demo finished that day and I didn't need the constant harassment from their asses.

"Let's get this shit done, before Sebastian wrings our damn necks."

"All right, I need to hear this demo of yours. If it's good, we'll re-record it tonight and pitch it to a few radio stations and clubs in the area by the weekend. Hope y'all are ready for this—this is what Metrix did and now look at them, they're on the Billboard Top 100 for what, eight weeks now? That could be Spasm one day."

Damn, I hadn't even thought that far ahead. I was just happy to be making music and having an agent in our corner; it had never crossed my mind to get to the top of the charts. *I need to dream bigger.* Hell, we all needed to.

Before we started, Dean called an emergency group meeting. He'd asked Sebastian and Tyrone if they could leave the room so we could have some privacy. "Guys, what do you truly want? What do you hope to achieve? Because if you commit to this now, our lives as we know it will forever be changed."

"There you go, being all responsible and shit." Reg chuckled.

Dean glared at him with a stern look. That look had the power to make water turn into ice, it was so cold. "I'm serious, dude."

"I'd love to walk into the mall and hear one of our songs blaring through the speakers as I shop. I'd love to get a call from Mel and hear that our music video has been showed a million times a day," Alexis said.

"I just want to make enough money to live comfortably, and I'll bust my ass to do so," Colt said.

"Cody, what about you?" Colt asked.

"I want it all. The fame, the fortune, the lavish fucking life. I want our music played everywhere. I want to perform at sold-out arenas, hearing our band's name chanted until people's throats give out. I'll do whatever it takes to get that. I need it."

"Then it's settled. Let's fucking do this. Spasm on international world tour is my dream. Guess we have a demo that needs to be played and re-recorded."

"Guys, these songs fucking rock! I don't have many complaints except the fact that I want a little more power from you Alexis, and Reg, you need to stop going ahead of the beat. Count slowly in your head as you hit your snares and you're golden."

We'd re-recorded three songs and I was ready to drop dead. It'd been hours and he'd made us start and stop so much that I wanted to stab him through the chest with the end of my guitar. I knew it'd be hard work to get this going, but damn, I didn't think I'd get sick of hearing my own songs before the world had gotten a chance to hear them. And we had seven more songs to do. *Kill me now.*

After the sixth song he sent us home for the night. "Holy shit, that was intense."

"I know, Colt, but we can do this. We have no choice, it's our dream, man. All the bands you idolized went through shit like this, or worse."

"Quit your bitching. Things will get worse before they get

better," Reg chimed in.

"Hopefully they get better soon because my fingers are sore from hitting the keys so much today."

"Well, pretty boy, you better go and play in the dirt for a while to toughen them up."

"Fuck you, Cody."

"No, fuck your hands and quit being a pansy. I've had calluses on my hands since birth because I've always been destined to play the guitar. So man the fuck up!"

He punched me in the chest and walked by with a smug smirk on his face. *That's what I thought.*

Chapter 30

CJ has been so busy with the band lately and it's made me feel slightly neglected. I knew what I was getting myself into, dealing with a rock star in the making, but I didn't realize things would be so hard already. Most nights he'd come over after hours of practice and would just go to sleep. It's nice to have him over, don't get me wrong, but it sucked that we haven't done anything as a couple. We hadn't even had sex lately. We ate out of the same plate the other day, so I guess that counts for some form of intimacy.

It took me a while, but I finally submitted an article to my professor. He confirmed he received it, but hasn't given me a grade yet. I'd been refreshing my email for days to see if he had anything to say, whether it was positive or negative. I knew the rise of Spasm would be a great piece and I'd hope he'd see it that way.

I'd applied online for several journalism internships and a few were interested in giving me interviews as soon as they got a letter of recommendation from my teacher. *There's always something.*

CJ had texted me and told me he was gonna be late that night and my heart sank in my chest. He'd promised me that the demo would be finished and we could order Chinese and just sit and drink because he'd have a break for the next few days. I was like a lovesick puppy, moping around all night after that.

Pen was out of town and I was so lonely.

As I wallowed in self-pity on the couch, watching every chick flick I could find on demand, there was a soft knock at the door. I looked over at the clock and it read eleven p.m.

"Who is it?"

"Chinese food delivery," a strange voice announced from the other side of the door.

I opened the door and peeped out with the chain still attached and there he was, with a huge brown bag in his hand and a bottle of wine in the other. "Surprise," he said, a sly grin spreading across his lips.

"You suck! I was so depressed after your text."

"I know, but you have to let me in or I'll take this all back home and eat there."

I slid the chain off the door and he wrapped his long arms around me. He smelled so good, like a tropical rain storm. He placed the food and wine down on the table and pulled me back into his embrace, kissing me on the top of my head. I felt our hearts beating at the same rhythm.

"CJ, I—"

"Shh, don't spoil the moment," he joked, placing my head back against his chest.

I backed out from his hold and slapped him on the chest. "Not cool, Jamison."

"What? You know how much I enjoy your company."

"That's it? What am I, your bestie or something?"

"No, but you're the best damn thing that's ever happened to me." He looked down at me with his sultry brown eyes and grasped either side of my face in his hands before placing a soft kiss on my lips. Kissing him made everything I'd questioned about us melt away.

We both stood still, silently staring into one another's eyes. There was nothing else to say, nothing else to be done, but I wanted to give all my love to him and I hoped he could feel the frequency of my heartbeat transmitting to him.

"Shannon, your stomach is rumbling, love, let's eat," he said, laughing aloud and bending down to grab the bag.

Chapter 31

I hated that we had to practice so much that I could barely spend any time with Shannon, but she understood what I had to go through, no matter how much it sucked. I'd lied to her that night because I wanted to see the smile on her face when I showed up at the door with the dinner and wine I promised.

It was a hell of a lot later than I wanted, but Sebastian had turned into some kind of fucking musical Nazi, yelling at us and screaming at us if we screwed up a bar, or if we were getting too tired of playing the same fucking scale over and over.

Dean somehow got us out of practicing for the weekend and I was going to make damn sure I spent most of it with her. My dick was in dire need of attention and it and my hand had a love-hate relationship at the moment.

"CJ?"

"Yeah, babe?"

"What's it like?"

"What's what like?"

"Actually going for your dream?"

"It sucks; I recommend you never try it at all." I laughed.

"No, I'm serious. Like, I can tell it's hard work, but you guys have a guide and with his help you'll skyrocket to the top, right?"

"I don't know, Shan. I mean, he's been working us so goddamn hard I don't know if I even want this anymore."

"Cody Jamison, don't say that! I'm sure it'll get easier, it has to, right?"

"I'll keep you posted. But, enough about me and my dreams, let's eat and make some dreams of our own."

After Shan and I shoved our faces, my phone blew up before I got a chance to slip my dick inside of her. I'd hit ignore, but apparently whoever it was didn't get the fucking memo.

"What?" I yelled into the phone, not giving a fuck about who was on the other line.

"CJ, it's me. Are you able to talk?"

"Red? What's going on?"

"Well, I've got some bad news."

My ears perked up. "What?"

"Well, Colt had a weird vibe about our new manager."

"And what kind of *vibe* was this?"

"Well, he told me that when we were recording our demo, he had some kind of device hidden in his hand. And every time he yelled at us to start over, he'd mess with it."

"Okay? Get to the point, Red."

"The asshole was stealing our material and leaking the shit online."

"Well, has it gotten any hits?"

"Oh yeah, but it's not us who are fucking singing it."

"What in the ever-loving fuck? How is that possible?"

"The bastard was recording our lyrics, and having some shitty second-rate band with auto-tune singing it and posted it online to make a profit."

"Can't we sue him or some shit?"

"I'm not sure. Ambrose is investigating it right now. We're still off for the weekend, but I'm gonna text you the link so you can check it out yourself. If Mel wasn't with me, I would have gone to his office and punched him square in his little dick."

"Aww that's cute, I didn't think you knew what a dick was."

"Fuck you, CJ. This is me being serious!"

"I know, and don't worry; Dean will get this shit in order."

"He'd better!"

I'd left Shannon in the room alone because I wasn't sure which way this conversation was going to go, but as soon as I came back, her eyes were full of questions that her lips hadn't asked yet.

"It was Red. Our manager is a snake bastard, and I'm gonna check out this website real quick on your laptop."

"Okay then. It's on the counter."

I grabbed the laptop and typed in the website Red texted me on my cell. And sure as shit, two of our songs were up. They'd changed the name of them, but they had thousands of fucking hits and we hadn't even performed them outside the studio yet.

"Oh, this asshole is going the fuck down, and I don't mean in a good way."

"What's going on?"

"Remember the demo we'd recorded in Reggie's studio?"

"Yeah."

"Well, two of the songs from our unreleased album are now online for the world to hear under some poser band's name, so unless we act fast, no one will know it's ours and we'll be royally fucked in the ass if we try to go public with this, because no one would believe us."

"That sucks."

"You don't even know the half."

It took a lot to piss me off: one, stealing my shit, and two, harming my girl. And since my music was just as personal as having a girl, I was doubly pissed and Sebastian's snake ass was going to pay.

Me: *Rico, I need a favor.*

Chapter 32

I'd only seen CJ that mad once before and that was when he felt I betrayed him. I promised to never do that to him again, but from the devious smile that spread across his lips as he texted someone on an all black phone, I knew something bad was going down.

A few weeks had gone by and suddenly Spasm wasn't as busy as they had been previously. CJ wouldn't answer any of my questions, but I knew deep down in my heart that something bad happened because I'd seen their old manager on the news. He'd gotten arrested for embezzling money, committing fraud, and illegally leaking his clients' music, breaking a dozen rules on the supposed iron-clad contracts they'd signed.

As much as I loved the newfound time we'd gotten to spend together, I could tell he was depressed. It must have sucked to have everything you'd ever wanted at your grasp and then get it snatched from your hand, bringing you right back to square one.

"So what happens now? Have you guys been working on a new demo or anything?"

"No, we loved that one, so we're shopping it around now, trying to find a new agent. You know, one that won't bend us over the table and take us from behind, raw, without any lube."

"I'm sure the next agent you find will shoot you guys to the top and Sebastian will just be a bottom bitch in jail."

"Oh my God, Shannon!"

"What?"

"What do you know about being a bottom bitch?"

"I do watch Netflix you know; I've binge-watched a few prison shows." I laughed.

"Well, I've got a new show for you to watch."

"And what might that be?"

"On Your Knees, by Cody Jamison," he said as he tried to push my head down to the front of his zipper. Playing along, I obliged, but not without putting up a fight.

"Or, On His Knees, starring Cody Jamison," I cracked, popping back up on my heels, and pushing his head toward my zipper.

"I can get down with that," he said, licking his lips.

Chapter 33

Within a few weeks we'd gotten interviewed by several different agents. Some promised us the world and others couldn't promise we'd get our demo played on the radio. But no matter how many we'd seen, none of them were good enough to represent Spasm. We were on our way home when Dean got a call on his cell. His face lit up like a kid on Christmas and I knew it was the news we'd been hoping for.

"Well?"

"Dude, that was Jerry Borough from State Records."

"And? What the fuck did he say?"

"He wants to represent us."

"Okay, well, what makes him so special?"

"Dude, he's the manager of Twisted Tyrant, the multi-platinum group."

"Holy fuck. Well, when do we see him?"

"Right now."

"At ten at night?"

"Yep. Kandy, here's the address," he said, slipping her a piece of paper he just so happened to have in his pocket. "I hope y'all are ready for this. If we can land Jerry, our lives will be fucking made!"

"Fuck yeah!" Reg said, slapping Colt on the back of his shoulder.

"If I wasn't so excited right now, I'd punch you in the fucking balls, man," Colt snapped.

It felt like we were on the road forever before we finally pulled up in front of this hexagon-shaped building, with illuminated lights on every single floor. "That's where we're going?" Alexis asked.

"Yeah, and I just got a text from Jerry. He said we can meet him on the fifth floor."

"Why do I feel like this is some kind of set-up? Dean, I'm sorry for whatever fucked up thing I've done."

He chuckled so hard, I could feel the vibrato from the seat behind me. "You're good, bro. I've been talking to him for a while, but I didn't want to say anything until I knew for sure."

"Gee thanks, way to keep us in the dark, asshole," Colt said.

"Remember how excited we all got about Sebastian? I didn't want the same shit to happen again. I didn't want to get everyone all schoolgirl excited, just to be let the fuck down."

"Touché."

Kandy parked in front of the building as we all hopped out. Colt ran ahead and yanked the handle to the enormous glass door, propping his body in front of it to let us all enter the building. There were two security guards inside, and they let us all pass through without so much as a single pat down.

One hit the button to let us in the elevator and we all nervously stepped inside and remained quiet as the golden box ascended to the fifth floor.

A tall guy, with long dark hair, a thick mustache, and a pair of jeans and a t-shirt, met us at the door and smiled. "You must be Spasm."

"Sure are."

"Well, step into my sound booth and let's get to business."

I looked at Dean and scratched my head, confused as fuck. "Wait a goddamn minute. What is going on here?"

"Seriously? I feel like this is moving a little too fast," Alexis chimed in.

"Listen, guys, you can trust Jerry. I promise you, he's not a snake-ass bastard like Sebastian was."

"Well, I still don't trust him as far as I can throw him. I'm watching you, Jerry."

"That's fine, but if you want your first single on the air tomorrow, you'd better watch your form and play the shit out of that guitar, Mr. Jamison."

"Wait, what? Tomorrow?"

"Tomorrow. Now let's get down to business."

We all walked into the sound booth, the brand new equipment taunting us as we all took our assumed positions behind the glass.

"Feel free to use and abuse this stuff, guys, it's all yours." Jerry's voice boomed over the speakers. An even taller guy joined him and started adjusting the slider up and down the mixing board.

"What song are we gonna do, Dean? If this is going to be our first single, I want it to be the shit."

"How about Standoff?"

"Hell yeah! Let's do it!"

The Standoff
I found you lying in the bathroom stall
Crimson splattered on the tiles and wall
Unresponsive, but the hope remained
That I was sleeping, this was all a dream
You've got to be strong, I don't care what people say
You've got to make it, you'll matter one day
You gave me life,
You've made things right,
Why did you do this?
We could have won this fight

The demons within, are cruel and harsh

Death is creeping, around the marsh

Breathe, you've got to make it

Breathe, I can't take it

Breathe, you're all I need

Breathe, take it all from me

Please, take it all from me

Speeding down the highway, no fucks given

I strapped you in tight, I hate to be alone

We're getting close, no time to stop now

I wish I'd feel your heart beat faster

I don't want to let go of you

Please don't go into the light

Red and blues flashing bright

No stopping now, I'll have to fight

Blood seeps into my leather, but the EMTs are here now, Heather

I wanna be with you every night and day, you've got to, you need to stay

Paddles charged, chest thumping up and down, please come back, you can turn your life around

Things look grim, but I have faith in you, and I have faith in him

Take a stand

Take a stand

The life regained through the pulse in your hand, those eyes once closed, were gazing at me, the boys in blue have handcuffed me, I fought through the crowd and said it loud

Standoff

This is a standoff

If you take her, you must take me too

I'm all she's got, she's screwed
It was all a mistake
Don't trap her in that place
She's mine forever this is a motherfucking standoff
If you take her, you've got to take me too
You've got to take me too

"Guys, that was fucking amazing! Now, let's go and talk contracts and all that other legal jargon."

When the dust settled, Jerry knew his shit. He knew this business like the back of his hand, and when he let us hear the play-back of Standoff, I almost came in my pants. We sounded like us, so real, so raw, and so fucking authentic. And right then, he won me over—hell, he won *us* over.

"I need you guys to come back here bright and early tomorrow morning. I want to re-record the rest of the songs on your demo. I don't want to be involved with any version that Sebastian touched. I'm here to enhance your sound, but I'm also gonna set shit straight. I am your business partner first, friend and manager second. I'll always have your needs in mind, and if something doesn't feel or smell right, we ditch it immediately. Cool?"

"Cool," we said simultaneously.

Me: I'm coming over, wear something sexy for me. Or nothing at all works too.

Shan: You're a pig, I'm not wearing anything, I just got out the shower.

Me: Good, see you in twenty.

We all piled up into the van and released a sigh of relief. "I have a good feeling about this guy. I can tell he doesn't take any shit, but he won't be a complete douche nugget at the same time," Alexis said.

Dean was being dropped off first, and I let him know that he shouldn't wait up for me. I didn't tell him I was going to fuck his sister, but he knew I was going to go and fuck someone.

I slid into Shannon's hot, wet, pussy, and buried myself so deep that she left claw marks on my back. That night was a fucking momentous occasion, and I wanted her to feel how thrilled I was.

Chapter 34

Practice after practice, hour after hour, we'd spent in that studio. We were there so much we decided to leave extra clothes and snacks behind so we wouldn't have to leave as often. Cutting a demo at home was a piece of cake, but cutting a demo in an actual professional studio, with a dedicated sound engineer and a hard-ass for a manager, proved to be much harder.

We were on the last song, "Confessions," one that I'd thought up out of thin air. Jerry said we should use it as a bonus song, but we all came to an agreement that it would be the second single we'd release after "Standoff."

As we wrapped up our practice, we decided to leave for the night and celebrate at Charlemagne's. Our presence there had been scarce lately and we were long overdue to have fun some with old friends. Once we walked through that old beaten-up door, there was a loud roar of applause. Personally, it scared the fuck out of me, but I couldn't let them know that.

"Okay, thanks, but what's the occasion?" Dean questioned.

"We heard you guys on the radio! Actually, they've been playing your song all day. It's been the most-requested single today!" a random groupie shouted.

Fuck, I'd forgotten all about that. We were so busy cutting this demo that we had totally forgotten about our single being released today. I knew Jerry was good, but he had just elevated himself to genie status. I hope we never, ever have to get rid of him.

"Well, I guess it's time to celebrate, now isn't it?"

"It's a celebration, bitches, let's drink!" Reg shouted.

We ordered a pitcher of beer and took our usual spots around the front of the bar. I'd gotten so wrapped up in this attention high that I'd forgotten to text Shannon. I pulled my phone out of my pocket and had a shit-ton of texts.

They all basically said the same thing, but different variations. Every time she heard the song she must have texted me. I felt like a dick for not responding, but tonight was a night to have carefree fun, and not have to worry about strings. "The rock star life is upon us!" I yelled into the crowd, clinking my mug of beer with absolute strangers.

> **Shannon:** *I'm so proud of you, CJ. I just heard your single on the radio and it gave me goose bumps.*
>
> **Me:** *Thanks.*

I'd gotten so drunk I couldn't even think straight. All I remembered was heading to the bathroom to take a piss and then my dick was out and some random bitch was on her knees in front of me. Who was I to say no?

Chapter 35

I knew CJ had been busy with the single releasing, and the demo recording, but I heard from Ambrose that they'd be at Charlemagne's to celebrate that night and I decided I was going to surprise CJ. I slid on the sexiest lingerie that I owned, a red teddy with no panties underneath, and wore a sexy dress that stopped mid-thigh. I didn't do slutty often, but I wanted to give him easy access.

As I made my way through the crowded bar, he was nowhere to be found. I circled around, looked in the offices and even asked around, but everyone was shit-faced at that point and couldn't give me clear direction. I'd decided to walk down the hall toward the bathrooms and heard loud banging and screaming.

I knocked on the door to make sure it was nothing serious, and what I saw before me made my stomach lurch and I dry heaved. CJ had two girls with him, they both had their skirts up and his dick was deep inside one as his fingers were inside the other. He seemed completely oblivious to the fact that I'd been standing there. I don't know what made me do it, but I walked over to him. One of the groupies asked if I wanted to tag in. "Hell no, I don't, and fuck you, Cody Jamison. Lose my number," I said as my fist connected with his jaw.

"Sh-Shannon?" he sputtered, too drunk to even finish his thought. I smacked him across the face with my open hand and stormed out of the room, running right past my brother. He saw how pissed I was, but I just kept moving; I didn't feel like explaining myself to him, or anyone else.

"I don't know why I thought he'd settle down for me, Pen. He's gonna be a fucking rock god, and little ol' hometown Shannon can't hold a candle to that."

"Shannon, I'm so sorry," she said, as she pulled me into her chest. "This life can't be an easy one and given the history between the two of you, what do you think you should do?"

"I don't know. Part of me wants to find him and cut his dick off, but the other part wants to fuck him until he realizes that he doesn't need anyone else, and that I'm enough woman for him."

"I'm not one to judge, but I think you need to follow your heart."

"My heart is conflicted at the moment, Pen. I wish you could have seen the look on his face when he saw me. It was like he looked right through me. He could barely get the word 'Shannon' out of his mouth."

"Send him a text, tell him he fucked up and maybe in the morning when the high wears off, he can explain his fucking actions."

"Okay. So what's going on with you and Reg?"

"The usual. I was gonna go celebrate, but I decided not to because, well, I didn't want to end up crying on your breasts."

"Good thing. I don't even know where he was."

"Probably in the stall next to CJ." We laughed, but it was bitter.

Was this what my life was going to be reduced to? Being a side groupie to the man I fell in love with when I was nine?

The next morning, I awoke to the sound of my phone blaring beside my head. *Ouch.*

"Hello?"

"Hey, is this Shannon?"

"Yes, who is this?"

"Raquel."

"Raquel who?"

"I'm one of the girls that was with Jamison last night, I'm calling to tell you to come and get him. He's fucked up and I'm done with amateur rock star wannabees that can't hold their ecstasy."

"Where are you?"

"I'll text you the place to meet me. He won't quit crying your name, so I looked through his phone and by the texts you guys have sent each other, I figured you were the 'Shannon' he was crying about."

When I see this girl, I'm going to choke the piss out of her.

"Pen, can I borrow your brass knuckles?"

"Whoa, what in the fuck is going on? It's a little early for brass knuckles."

"I have to go and get CJ, and possibly punch a girl in the face. I haven't decided yet."

"Shan, you can't go busting in skulls every time the mistress calls or texts you."

"Like hell I won't."

"I'm coming with you for backup, and to record this. This should be good."

My head pounded in my ears as I drove to the address the girl had given me. I had the worst hangover, but getting CJ was more important than getting aspirin. I felt like he was in trouble and didn't want him staying a minute longer with that stupid girl.

As I pulled up in front of a rundown shack, she emerged in her bra and panties, pointing to the opened door.

"Really? You're a classy one, aren't ya?"

"Yep, I'll see you in nine months when I give birth to his baby. He gave it to me raw, all night."

I snapped. Completely lost it. I lunged at the brunette, wrapping my hands around her throat, watching her blue eyes bug out of her head. "You stupid bitch, you will not be having his baby if I have anything to do with it!" I punched her in the stomach repeatedly until Penelope dragged me off of her.

"Shan, she's not worth it, you need to go and see if CJ is still alive in there. This place looks—and smells—like shit." She pinched her nose closed as she tightly linked her arm with mine to keep me focused on the task at hand.

We stormed up the broken stone steps and saw a pair of men's jeans laying across the floor. "CJ? Are you in here?" A muffled gurgle came from behind a closed door. We tried to open it, but it was locked. "CJ, it's me, Shannon. If you're in there, please unlock the door so Penelope and I can take you home."

"I'm naked. That bitch wouldn't give me my clothes back."

"I found your pants, let me in and you can put them on. Pen, stay here, just in case nutty Nancy decides to come back for more."

"You got it, chief," she said, taking the brass knuckles from me.

I heard the tumbler unlock and slid in the room swiftly, as to not let anyone else see CJ naked. There was a dim light coming from the mirror above the filthy sink, and he was sitting on top of the toilet. His hair was a mess, his eyes were glossy, and dark black and blue circles surrounded them.

"CJ, what happened?"

"I don't know, Shannon. One minute I was drinking beers with the band, and the next I was here. I don't remember a fucking thing that happened, but my balls, dick, and fingers hurt. So I'm assuming there was a hardcore night of fucking that I—" He stopped mid-sentence. Sadness consumed his once-powerful stare. "Wait a minute, you were there. You came into the bathroom when I'd lost total control. Or was I hallucinating?"

"I was there. I came to surprise you at the bar, and well—it didn't go as planned."

"Shannon, I am so fucking sorry. You know I'd never purposely hurt you, not like this."

"I know, but it's still like a knife in my chest. It made me realize that I'm not ready for this life, CJ. I'm happy for you, but I can't go another night wondering what you're out there doing, with God knows who. I don't want to have to come and rescue you from some overnight binge again. Do you realize that woman out there is hoping to have your baby? God only knows what kind of diseases she might have. I can't do this again. I'll drop you off at your apartment, and then I think I'll need to take a break from you, CJ."

"Shannon, no. I don't want anyone else, you're it."

"Save it, CJ. We've been through this before and I'm sick of hearing it. Consider this your wake-up call. I can't do this anymore."

Chapter 36

There were no words to express the heartbreak that washed over Shannon's face that day. She was already fragile, a box full of glass, waiting to be displayed and properly handled, and I stomped on that box and broke every single piece inside.

The ride back to my apartment was quiet, and every time she glanced at me through the rearview mirror, my insides hurt like hell. There was no coming back from this, no fucking way she'd be able to forgive me and stay by my side. I couldn't promise her the world, when I only had the city to offer. She deserved more, and I knew then that I had to let her go.

She dropped me off in front of the building without a single goodbye and I couldn't blame her. I wouldn't speak to me either. I walked through the door and Dean and the band were sitting on the couch.

"Dude, you had us fucking worried sick," Colt shouted, running to give me a hug and then backing away. "You could use a shower, though."

"What the hell happened? One minute you were fine, then the next you were speaking gibberish and some weird foreign girls were pulling you away from us."

"They slipped me something and I practically blacked out. I don't know what the hell happened, but I never want to go through this ever again."

"Good, well, Jerry wants to see us at the studio in an hour, so go and get changed."

Fuck, that's the last thing I wanted to do.

My head hurt so fucking much that after a quick shower and a fresh change of clothes, I popped ibuprofen like candy and grabbed the darkest shades I could find to shield the blinding sun from my sensitive eyes.

Every noise echoed and made my ears and head ring. "Guys, can you keep it down?"

"We're not talking, it's the radio," Kandy said.

"Ugh, this is something I'd like to never experience again. Reg, I don't know how the fuck you recover from this, but fuck, I can't do this again."

Kandy dropped us off and we made our way to Jerry's office. He met us at the door and smiled so big I thought his teeth would drop out of his mouth. "There's the best thing to ever happen to me!" he said as he shoved us all into his office.

I took a seat on the corner of the long leather sectional as the others sat as close to him as they could.

"Have you guys heard your song on the radio?"

"No, everyone told us how much it played yesterday, but we never thought to actually turn the damn thing on and listen for ourselves. Why the hell didn't we turn it on?" Dean said.

"You guys shattered records yesterday. Your song was the most-requested single in the last ten years. Standoff was playing on multiple stations. You guys are going to go far. We need to talk and figure out how big you guys want to go. I'll give some suggestions, but I can't force you to do anything you don't want to do, that's never been my style."

"Right now I just want to fucking sleep."

"Quit your bitching, we have to think about our future and if you're incapable, we'll decide for you," Reg said.

"Go right the fuck ahead."

After the unexpected hour we'd spent in Jerry's office, we were all sort of on the same page. I just agreed to everything that was thrown at me, because I didn't give a fuck.

I was too worried about Shannon. I couldn't wrap my head around what went through her mind when she saw me last night. Fucking two bitches, when she thought I was hers. Hell, I am hers, always have been, but I have to figure out my life. *Fame, fortune, and bitches? Or fame, fortune and the love of my life?*

I'd managed to slip away from the band for a minute and called Shannon, but as I suspected, she'd sent me to voicemail every time.

> **Me:** *Shan, I'm sorry. I really need to talk to you.*
>
> **Shan:** *She doesn't want to talk to you, fuck off.*

Okay, I deserved that.

For weeks I couldn't get a hold of her. I guess she decided to block my number and I couldn't fucking blame her. Everything felt like it was all going to shit for me, when I should have been on cloud nine.

The band could tell I was off, because I wasn't feeling anything we played. I couldn't write any new lyrics, hell, my dick wouldn't get hard I was so depressed.

"CJ?" Alexis whispered. "Can I talk to you for a minute?"

"Sure." I followed her into an empty room at the end of the hall. I'd never noticed it before, but we hadn't gotten out of the studio much.

"I know you fucked up with Shannon, obviously big, by the widening of your eyes, but you've got to use that shit. Use that fire, that rage burning in your belly, and fuel your mind with the lyrics and spit them out on paper. We need you. Eventually she'll come back. They always come back."

"I don't know, Red. This wasn't a slap-on-the-wrist kind of fuck up. It was a my-dick-was-in-another pussy. I was blasted out of my fucking mind and she walked in and caught me."

"Fuck, dude! Okay well, again, use that shit. You can do it! 'Confessions' will thank you for it, trust me."

"All right, I'll try."

"You'd better." She tapped me on my crotch and kissed me on the cheek.

"Tease."

"You know it! Now get to work, asshole!"

The rest of the band decided to go out for drinks, and I decided to walk my ass home from the studio and get out of this funk I have going on.

My legs and back hurt like hell when I finally reached the front steps of our apartment, but I gave no fucks. I went inside, grabbed some water, and some pain pills. Sat my ass down on the couch, plugged my headphones into Dean's laptop and blasted whatever loud adrenaline-pumping playlist he had saved.

Confessions. "Come on, you can do this!" I yelled, slapping myself on the leg. I cracked my knuckles, opened Word and after letting the sounds of Death Pain blare through the phones, I was golden. It all came to me. *This is going to be a fucking hit!*

Chapter 37

Everywhere I went, I saw posters of them. His eyes bore through my soul, even though they were fixed in the picture. I could still feel him around me. *I still wanted him to be around me.*

Penelope blocked his number on my phone and at first, I was okay with it, letting the days go by without seeing his name flash across my screen, but then I missed it. *I missed him.*

He's an adult, as am I, but I do believe he's to blame for his own actions. But being away from him made me think of the good ol' days. The days when we were young and innocent, sweet and kind.

"Shan, you look like a love sick puppy," Pen said, nudging me with her elbow.

"I am. When I'm not with him all I can think of are the good times, when he lived next door. Before all the sex and the heartache. When it was real."

"It's still real, it is so fucking real that you want to unblock his number and jump on his dick right now, right?"

"I hate you so much."

"You love me! Now pass me a piece of chicken, mama bear is hungry."

"Pen, you don't think I'm an idiot for wanting to forgive him, do you?"

"No, that entire band is fucked in the head, so someone has

to love them. I do believe you need to set some ground rules though, because I have no desire to witness a Shan-attack ever again!"

"Okay, well, unblock his number before I go on the prowl on your butt right now! Meow!" *No, I couldn't figure out how to unblock it. I know, it's sad.*

"Here you go, kitten! Go get your man!"

> **Me:** It's me, CJ. We need to talk.
>
> **CJ:** I thought I'd never hear from you again.
>
> **Me:** Meet me at my place tonight.
>
> **CJ:** I'll be there.

"CJ, can you help me with something?"

"Sure. What do you need?"

"Can you help me climb this tree?"

"Shannon, do you not remember what happened the last time?"

"Yes, but I need to do this."

He bent down on one knee and weaved his fingers together so I could step into his hand before I climbed the tree. Boosting me up, I jumped as hard and as high as I could and grabbed the branch closest to me. I stuck my foot in the holes, not over-thinking, and sat on the branch. "I did it!"

"I knew you could, Shannon. You've got a lot of fire and determination inside that huge brain of yours."

"Are you saying I have a big head?"

"Me? No!" *He laughed. I could never get tired of it, and I could never get tired of him. I'd forgive him for anything, just for being my friend.*

"Friends always forgive."

"But they never forget."

"Let go of the pain."

"Let go of the regret."

"Listen, Shan, I'm sorry I—"

"Friends always forgive."

"But they never forget."

"Let go of the pain."

"Let go of the regret. Bet you thought I forgot our little saying, huh, Shan?"

"I definitely didn't think you'd remember." A tear escaped from my eye when he recited our old chant with me. It was the way we moved on from something that hurt us, and promised not to speak about it again. This was a different scenario, but the same rules applied. I could never stay mad at him, even if I tried. Maybe I was stupid, and naïve, but he's the one I want and I'd do anything to have him.

He walked toward me, his chest heaving up and down, the hesitance showing in his stare. "I want to kiss you, Shannon."

"Then do it."

He stepped forward, closing the gap between us and ran his thumb across my lips. "Not now, I don't deserve it. Let me earn the right to kiss you. Let me earn the right to make you mine."

Chapter 38

She was ready. Willing. She wanted to let me in, but I didn't deserve it. I couldn't keep fucking this girl over. I promised myself I wouldn't do that shit again, and I did. Even if it wasn't entirely my choice, I still screwed up and the thought of her seeing it went through my mind almost daily.

Things were different with her; they'd always been different. I never figured it out, until now, and it's because she's always had the key to my heart.

"All right, guys and girl, I have some great news for you."

"What is it?" Alexis asked.

"Well, I've booked a few practice gigs for you. Now that you've been on the radio, more venues will be willing to book you for dirt-cheap prices."

"Why so cheap?"

"Because they can boost their ticket prices as high as they want, but that's not the point of this conversation. Every week you'll be in a new city, and I've seen the busted van you're riding in, if you need to upgrade, or need a tune-up let me know as soon as possible. I don't need you guys getting maimed on the side of the road by fans."

"I'm down."

"Good. Now that your demo is tight and polished, you have

a lot more work to do. You have to promote yourselves, on social media especially. That's where all your fans are. That's where the extra revenue will come from."

"I hate being online," Reg groaned.

"I can imagine. I just need one of you to tweet or snap something once a day about what the band is up to, that's it. Maybe post a picture. Trust me, the more personal you guys get, the better. Fans love to see the softer side of musicians. It makes you seem more relatable."

"Can someone help us set it up and give us some pointers?" Colt asked.

"Absolutely, not only do I have the best radio connections, I have the best marketing connections as well. Spasm will take the internet by storm! Watch out world, here they come!"

At some point in time, my mind drifted elsewhere. I didn't feel like hearing this bullshit and decided to mess with Shannon.

Me:	*Fuck me.*
Shannon:	*What's wrong?*
Me:	*No I literally meant fuck me ;)*
Shannon:	*Pig, go and finish whatever it is that you're doing!*
Me:	*I wish I were doing you.*
Shannon:	*You haven't earned that yet.*
Me:	*Ouch, my heart is broken.*
Shannon:	*Ur heart is made of steel, nothing can break it.*
Me:	*You could.*
Shannon:	*But I won't—ever.*
Me:	*Good.*

Chapter 39

Cody

Unknown Caller: *We've found you, Jamison.*

Me: *Who the fuck is this?*

Unknown Caller: *Your debt will be paid with your life.*

Me: *Ok, fuck you weirdo.*

Since we'd picked up more gigs, I'd gotten all kinds of weird threats and texts on my phone. I figured they were just from groupies Reg gave my number to as a joke, but this recent one freaked me out a bit. I hadn't heard from Rico in a long time, so I thought everything was okay. Boy was I wrong.

As I sat in the apartment, trying to clear my head and think of a new song for the band to perform, my phone rang. It wasn't the one I use every day; it was the burner phone Rico had given me.

"Hello?"

"CJ, you're in trouble. I've been tracking those assholes all the way from Canada. I don't know how they were able to find you, but they're close. Do you have any shows coming up?"

"Fuck, I have one tomorrow night."

"Okay, text me the address, I'll make sure I'm around."

"Are you sure there's nothing else you can do to deter them or something?"

"Nah, I've kept them away from you this long, but somehow

they were able to find you. These bastards are resilient."

"Shit, no one knows what's going on and I don't want to put the band in danger."

"You'll have to tell them, CJ."

"I can't, I can't even tell—her."

"Anyone you know and care about will be put in danger; you need to let them know what's up."

"Okay, well, make sure you bring the guys to watch the venue."

"I'll do everything I can, I promise. Hey, CJ?"

"Yeah?"

"I'm sorry to tell you this, but your parents are dead."

"Fuck!"

For the first time in my life I was truly afraid. Not only for myself, but for everyone else I'd come in contact with. I thought once I'd crossed the border that I'd be fine—I wouldn't have to deal with this shit anymore. But I guess this is what I get for taking on a debt I knew I couldn't pay. A debt I didn't deserve to pay.

Every noise I heard in the apartment sent chills down my spine. I was never one to live in fear, but this shit was really getting to me. I didn't want to risk having Shannon over, but I needed to lay it all out there for her.

Me:	*Hey, I need to see you tonight.*
Shannon:	*Sure, your place or mine?*
Me:	*Yours.*
Shannon:	*K see you then.*

I knew it was a gamble going to Shannon's house, but I figured if I got there in one piece, they hadn't found me just yet. I needed to warn her without scaring the fuck out of her in the process.

As I walked up the familiar steps, I cautiously looked over

my shoulder to make sure I wasn't followed. I was getting ready to retreat back down them and take another lap around, but Shannon must have heard me and opened the door, stopping me dead in my tracks.

"CJ? Where are you going?"

"Hey, nowhere, I was just—"

"Are you all right? You look like you've seen a ghost or something."

I wish that was all it was.

"Shan, I have to tell you something." I ran my hand through my hair and escorted her to the couch.

"Okay, you're freaking me out. What's wrong? Are you sick?"

"Well, not exactly."

"Well, what is it?"

"Okay, if I tell you this, will you promise not to freak out?"

"I can't promise you anything, you're scaring me." Her legs bounced up and down as she looked at me with those sad, puppy dog eyes she's had since she was a kid.

"Remember when I kind of told you about the mob stuff before?"

"Not really, because you didn't really tell me anything."

"Well, they're coming after me."

"What? How do you know that?"

"A friend."

"What did you do, CJ?"

"I took on my father's old debts. My father gambled away all of his savings, the house we were staying in, and almost all of our possessions. In order for them not to kill him for lack of payment, when I was of age, about sixteen, my life changed forever. I had to work for them, at one of their chop shops. I was just the errand boy. I'd go and scout out cars, watch the owner and then report back when the coast was clear so they could go and steal it. I hated it so much. Then as I got older, they sent me on more dangerous missions."

"Like what?"

"Well I had to rob people at gunpoint, and then steal their cars and take them to the shop. I couldn't go through with it anymore. My friend used to be a part of it, too, but he would hack into people's accounts and wire money to offshore bank accounts for them. They thought he disappeared after the last job, but he didn't. We were both planning to leave, and once it was okay, he got me out of the country. He's been tracking them the entire time, and somehow they've found me."

"Well, how do you know it's not your 'friend'?"

"Because he wouldn't do that to me, he'd risk giving up his location and that wouldn't be smart for either of us. He's wanted by them more than I am."

"Okay, but I don't understand how you robbing people was paying your debts."

"The cars I would steal were worth a lot of money. They were luxury cars: Lamborghinis, Porsches, Corvettes, etc. They would chop the cars and sell all the parts. Whatever the car was worth, they'd deduct the price from the overall debt. I couldn't be a part of it anymore, Shan. I felt like I was selling my soul to the devil."

"Do I even want to know how much debt your father acquired?"

"No, you don't. It'd take the rest of my life, or, if I had a kid, it'd be passed on to them and I couldn't do that."

"Oh my God, this is just—hard to process."

"I know, but I'm afraid if they find me, they'll kill me and everyone else that I love."

"What do you mean everyone else?"

"They killed my parents."

"I—" I silenced her with a kiss, because if this was the last night I got to feel her from the inside, I was gonna make it fucking count.

Chapter 40

When his lips crashed against mine, I felt the hunger from within his soul. He was scared and if this were the last time I'd see him, I wanted it to be something to remember. I'd never seen him look that spooked about anything in my life.

"CJ," I said, breaking the kiss.

"Yeah?"

"Are you going to warn the band? And are you okay?"

"I don't know. It took a lot for me to tell you. It sucks about my parents, but there's nothing I can do," he said, reclaiming the crook of my neck with his tongue. "If something happens to me tomorrow, just know that I love you, Shannon, with everything in my soul. You're it for me. You've always been it for me."

Tears pooled in the corners of my eyes, as he lifted me off the couch and brought me back to my bedroom. He gently placed me on the bed and stood, staring at me. He unfastened his belt and unhooked his button, letting his pants fall to the ground. Kicking them off, he then tore his shirt over his head and continued to stare at me. It was like his eyes were telling me a story his body was going to write. He was the ink and I was the paper, waiting for the magic to happen.

He grabbed hold of my foot and roughly tugged me to the bottom of the bed. He kneeled down in between my legs and yanked my boy shorts to the floor. His tongue traveled from my inner thigh, flicked over my clit and down my other thigh, then back up to my clit. Circle after circle, he traced around the bud, before he picked up the pace and clasped his jaw around me.

Passion seared through my body, tears of pleasure fell from my eyes, and I felt a fire building within, an orgasm was erupting through me. This was the strongest one I'd ever had with him. Ripple after ripple tore through my core, my body continuously seized from his touch, but he wouldn't stop. Flicking, licking, fingering, sucking—he was determined to drink me until there was nothing left to sip.

I tried to push his head away due to the extreme sensitivity I was experiencing, but he wasn't ready to stop until my body stopped reacting to his touch. He broke his hold and we looked at each other for a moment, and I swore his brown eyes had turned black.

His boxers had come off at some point and as he pressed his cock at the apex of my thighs, I writhed in a little pain from being so sensitive. "Not tonight, Shannon. I can't be gentle tonight," he growled.

"CJ, you need to put a condom on."

"Are you serious?"

"I don't want any disease you may have caught from that girl." He tapped me on the thigh and bent down to retrieve a condom from his pocket.

"Point taken."

He slammed inside of me and I came undone. There was nothing left, nothing else to give; he'd claimed every part of me from the inside out. I'd forgotten what it felt like to have someone completely brand you from the inside and he'd put his mark everywhere.

I couldn't sleep a wink that night. I was paranoid and so sore from the domination of Cody Jamison. He was continuously switching back and forth between two phones and freaking out more and more. I wanted to ask him what was going on, but I didn't feel like it was my place.

"CJ, don't you have to practice soon?"

"Yeah, but things have gotten a lot worse."

"How so?"

"Well, there's an official hit out on me, so I'm almost guaranteed to die."

Oh my God, no. This can't be happening. He can't die. It would shatter my entire existence.

"I don't know what to say," I cried, unable to see from the tears blurring my vision.

"Shannon, it's okay. I always knew there was a possibility this could happen."

"But I didn't. I can't lose you again!" I punched and slapped at his chest, clawing at his bare skin, marking my territory. "If they take you, they'll have to take me too."

"Shannon? Where are you, honey?"

"Over here," I cried as I pressed my head back against the Jamison's back door.

"Oh, baby girl, what's wrong?"

"I miss him, Mom. He wasn't just Amby's best friend, he was mine, too."

"I know, but this is the third time this week I've found you over here, honey. This isn't healthy." She looked at me with her hand on her chin.

No one understands me. I might be ten, but CJ was everything to me. He was the stick to my Popsicle, the sprinkles to my favorite ice cream. Nothing makes sense without him.

"Mom, I don't know what to do. He wasn't supposed to leave like that. I haven't even heard from him. He promised, Mom! He promised!" I slammed my fists on the steps and the tears kept falling.

"Let me tell you a little something about boys. Most times they tell the truth, but other times, they promise things they know deep down they can't keep."

"Does Daddy do that?"

"All the time," she said, as she wiped the fresh tears from the

corners of my eyes.

I know that was supposed to make me feel better, but it didn't. It only made things worse.

"Mom, can you just go? Leave me alone for five more minutes. I promise I won't try to break in again, I just want to sit here."

"Five minutes. I'll send Ambrose over to come and get you. But I want you to know something. I know you and CJ had some kind of puppy love, but you will get over this. I promise. You'll find someone else that won't let you hurt like this."

"It's not puppy love! It's true love, Mom! You'll see! And there will never be anyone else—ever!"

A month had gone by and I would still occasionally sit on the steps in front of the abandoned Jamison house. I couldn't let go. None of this made sense to me. I cuddled with the gifts he'd given me every night, and one night things got a little easier. I stopped thinking about him as hard and Amby helped me do something to let out the anger I was feeling—I joined the junior track team at my school. It was easy to run and keep my mind focused on something other than CJ.

"Shan, this will help you feel better, I promise."

I can't let another boy do this to me again, this is nuts.

"Shannon, no. You can't say shit like that, this is my family's fuck up and you will not get caught up in the crosshairs. Please don't come to the show tonight, okay? Promise me?" He walked toward me, grasping my shoulders tightly with his big firm hands. "Promise me, dammit!" he yelled, snapping me back to reality.

My tongue felt like it was tied in knots. I couldn't lie to him. I was going to come to the show whether he wanted me there or not. "CJ, I have to tell you something."

"What is it?"

"I have a sex tape."

"What? You?"

"Yeah, I made it with my ex and he uploaded it to this amateur porn website, and now millions of horny douche bags have seen my body."

"Oh my God. Please tell me your face isn't on it."

"No, he wasn't that stupid, but I was completely wasted and hadn't realized what was going on until he'd texted me the link the next day. Then he told me the fuck was nice, and now I'd be a star."

Rage built in his eyes and his knuckles were turning white from being clenched together so tightly. "I'll kill him."

"Don't worry, Ambrose already tried to."

"Obviously he wasn't successful. If I make it out of this hit alive, I'm going to find him and kill him, Shan."

"CJ, I can't let you do that! You'll get arrested, or worse—deported!"

"Fuck!"

Even though it wasn't a good time, someone besides Penelope and my brother needed to know. I had no idea how my brother even found out about the incident. I got the call from the bar Pen used to work at to come and get him before the police were called. He'd beaten my ex until his face had been unrecognizable, hence the scars on his hands.

"Shan, I have to go. Please don't come to the show tonight." His tongue slid down my throat, and he palmed my butt in his hands.

"I love you."

"I love you too, Shan."

I'm going to that show whether he likes it or not.

> **Me:** Mom, I just want you to know that I love you.
>
> **Mom:** I love you too, hon. Is something wrong?
>
> **Me:** I just wanted you to know, let Dad know too.
>
> **Mom:** I will. Is CJ okay?
>
> **Me:** No, but I don't want to talk about it.

Mom: *Ok, well, keep in touch. It's been a while since we talked.*

I couldn't promise her that. So I didn't.

Chapter 41

I'd been on edge all day. I was hopped up on caffeine and smoked a joint with Reg to calm the fuck down. No one besides Shannon knew what was going on and I planned on keeping it that way. I hoped she would do what I asked and keep her ass at home. I didn't need to worry about anyone else's safety. I just wanted to play this gig, get away safely, and then I'd tell the band what was going on.

As I worked the neck and strummed my guitar with my fingers, I could feel the song taking over. The song Standoff was something I cherished. I wrote it in my parents' basement six years ago and I never thought in a million fucking years that I'd be on stage at a paid concert with four of the best goddamn friends I could ask for, rockin' out.

Nothing could ruin this high, even the imminent threat I knew that could come and take my life away at a moment's notice. The crowd was cheering on their feet. The adrenaline was flowing through my fucking veins. This is it. This is everything I'd hoped and dreamed of. The blood, sweat, tears, and sacrifices were all worth it for this moment.

After Red sang the last low note, she told the crowd goodnight. The lights dimmed as we exited the stage and my bandmates and I, drenched in sweat, looked at our manager, Jerry, who looked very pleased on the sidelines.

"We rocked the shit out of that stage!" Reg crowed.

"Best performance ever!" I yelled over the crowd, who were still chanting our name.

"It felt so good to sing that in front of a sold-out stadium. I could sing that song every day as long as we got paid!" Alexis added.

"Hey, CJ?" Amber the stage hand, interrupted.

"Not now, Amber."

"But—"

"Amber, whatever it is it can wait! Guys, I'm gonna go grab a drink." Nothing could fade this feeling of euphoria I was feeling. I got the band, the money, the girl, the life I've always wanted, and nothing could take that away from me. Or so I thought.

I walked down the narrow hallway, sliding my guitar around my shoulders and stopped to admire the big black door with the gold star on it covered in big white letters that read Spasm. I will never get tired of that. I opened the door.

Boom.

Inhale.

Exhale.

Boom.

Inhale.

Exhale.

Boom.

Two breaths were all I remembered taking as a group of guys in black trench coats walked over my body, briefly gazing down at me before they walked out of the room. My life was draining out onto the shiny concrete floor. I pictured Shannon's sweet face and everything faded to black.

Chapter 42

"CJ. Wake up! Please."

I sat by his bedside, hot tears falling from my eyes, as I ran my hand gently up and down his left arm. I'd been at his side since they brought him here several days ago. It hurt seeing the man I'd loved for most of my life lying in front of me, fighting for his survival.

CJ had told me about the trouble his family had with the mob. He told me they were coming, but I didn't think things would go down like this. He told me he wasn't afraid to die. Even during the chaos that erupted after the sound of bullets echoed through the theater, I didn't tell anyone. I deleted everything off my laptop that he'd told me before, because I couldn't ruin us. His trust was more important to me than anything else. I'd slowly regained it back, and it wasn't worth losing him forever.

The past few months, CJ had lived the carefree rock star life and hadn't had any inkling that they were coming for him, until a few days before. He'd fled Canada months ago, but I guess no matter where you were, if you owed the mob a debt, they were going to find you.

"Shannon, what the hell are you doing here?" Ambrose barked.

"Keeping an eye on CJ, is that all right with you?"

His eyes turned dark and I could see the rage building with the flare of his nostrils. He looked just like our dad. "No. It's not. What if the assholes that did this to him came back to finish the job? Did that ever cross your mind?"

"Shut the hell up, Ambrose! I'm not a little girl anymore. I can do whatever the fuck I want and I can handle myself just fine! You don't think I'm not afraid? You don't think I know my life could be on the line at this very moment, for being in this hospital room? I do and guess what? I don't care!" *Shit.* I'd never talked to him like that before and his raised eyebrows and hanging bottom lip showed he was just as shocked as I was.

"Wow. Sorry—sis—this whole thing with CJ has us all on edge. We don't know who the fuck would want to hurt him. And I can't handle the idea of you getting hurt."

"I think everything will be okay."

"How do you know that?"

"I just know."

CJ had sworn me to secrecy, but he had someone following him to secure his safety. And in the event something did happen to him, that person was good to go after the assholes that harmed him. After I'd heard the bullets, I ran out back and that's when it all went down. Four men in long, dark trench coats and fedoras were laughing and speaking a foreign language as they climbed into an unmarked black SUV. I was frantically trying to get a license plate number when they turned the ignition switch and the SUV transformed into a fireball, shooting high in the sky.

I told CJ when I got there that night, but I don't know if he heard me. I had so much to tell him when he came out of his coma.

It tore me apart seeing him like this. Bandages covered his entire midsection. His dark hair was matted down on his head, a breathing tube was secured in his mouth and machine wires were connected to every part of his arms.

Ambrose joined me by his bedside and placed his hand on top of CJ's. "We canceled the tour indefinitely."

"Oh my God, Ambrose, why?"

"Because Spasm isn't Spasm, without him." For the first time in a long time, I saw tears forming in the corners of my brother's eyes. He cared about CJ like he was a part of our family. As did I, but that family boundary became something even more powerful the first time we made love.

"Amb—" It was on the tip of my tongue. I wanted to tell him then, that CJ and I were together, but I couldn't. I fought with myself internally, but I couldn't let the words fall off my tongue.

"What is it, Shannon?"

"I love you."

"Love you too, kid."

The nurse came into the room to check CJ's vitals. His heart rate and breathing were normal. His blood pressure had risen a little since she'd come in before. "You must be his girlfriend," the nurse said, a smug grin across her face.

I choked on air, as my brother laughed hysterically. "Not a fucking chance."

I remained silent as the nurse flashed knowing eyes at me. His laugh abruptly stopped and his dark eyes cut over to me.

"No way. My best friend and my little sister? If he doesn't die from this, I'm going to kill him myself."

"And what good will that do? I love him, Ambrose and he loves me too."

"I noticed he'd been different and cleaned up his act, but I'd never thought he'd betray me. I told you how I felt about this years ago, and it still stands now."

"I was nine years old! You could have told me the sky was green and I would have believed and trusted anything you'd said! But now, I'd give my life to be with him, Ambrose, just like I would for you. That's how important he is to me. One day you'll let a girl get under that hard exterior of yours and you'll find love, and when you do, you'll understand how I feel."

His intense stare softened, and he wrapped his arm around me. "CJ really did a number on you huh?"

"CJ always had my number; it never belonged to anyone else."

"I know. I remember how hard it was when he left. You have no idea how hard that was for me to see you falling apart at the seams and there was nothing I could do to help you. I hated feeling like that, Shan. As an older brother, it's my job to protect and comfort you, and I couldn't. I just don't want to see you hurt like that ever again."

The thought had never crossed my mind. I never took it into consideration how my actions affected the ones around me. Now I understood his opposition to our relationship. "I'm sorry, but let's hope he doesn't leave either one of us again."

"Let's hope not."

I'd fallen asleep by CJ's side, and Ambrose and the rest of his bandmates had come and gone. I couldn't fight back the tears as I looked him over, lying in the bed, helpless and still. The few days of stubble that had been perfectly lined on his face was now a full-grown beard. His hair was growing over his ears, and he didn't even look like the same person anymore. I'd give anything for him to open his eyes; those eyes were the key to my heart. They whispered to my soul, claiming the intricate parts of me that were always his.

"Shannon?" I heard from behind with a soft knock on the door. I turned around to see Jerry, their manager.

"Hey, Jerry."

"How's our boy doing?"

"The same. I just wish he'd open his eyes for me."

"Shannon, when's the last time you were home?"

"I don't know."

"I think you should let me sit with him for a while. Go home and rest, hon. If anything changes I'll call you right away, I promise."

Part of me didn't want to leave his side, but I needed a break, I missed my bed, and I was long overdue for a shower. I sighed.

"Okay, Jerry. If his hand twitches, you'd better call me."

"I will, I promise." When I'd first met Jerry, I could tell he genuinely cared about these guys. They'd gone through a lot, but he became their knight in shining armor.

I stood over CJ and ran my fingers through his hair once more and placed a kiss on his cheek. "I'll be back, CJ, please wake up." I paused to see if he'd respond, but he hadn't. "I love you."

A tear slid down my face and onto his arm. I wished it'd woke him up like a fairytale, but it hadn't, so I continued to the lobby to try and catch a cab home.

Once I'd gotten home, I felt sick to my stomach. It didn't feel like home without him in it. I plopped down on my couch in the dark, curling up into a ball around the couch pillow. It was the only thing I had that had remnants of his smell on it and I drifted off to sleep.

A few more weeks had gone by and CJ was still in a coma. His brain had started to swell from the blow to the back of his head, and they had to drill a small hole in his skull to help drain the fluid. In order to drill the hole, they had to shave off his hair on the left side. I had asked if I could just shave it all, because I'd hate to see him lying there with a half-head of hair.

I'd asked my brother to trim his beard up, because being that close to his face and getting no response from him made me shed tears every time. I felt like a part of me was dying right along with Cody. "CJ, come back to me," I whispered in his ear. "Please."

"Shannon, there's nothing we can do, hon. You heard the nurses. No one can get in contact with his parents, so he's basically stuck as a vegetable, until he either dies on his own or someone pulls the plug."

"How could you say that? Have you lost hope already? Are you ready to move on with your stupid fucking band and just leave him here to wither away? He helped you build that damn band, he's responsible for a shit-ton of your hit songs, and you dare sit here and say this to me? I don't even know you anymore, you're a damn monster!" I tossed the clipboard at him and waited for his rebuttal.

"Shan, I didn't mean it like that. I love him like a brother and you know damn well there will be no Spasm without him, but I hate to see what's happening to you. It's like when he left all those years ago. You've gone crazy, giving up your life because of him. You don't need to sit in here, confined in these four walls with him day after day. I assure you, the nurses will call you if anything changes."

Tears slid down my face, and as I balled my hand up into a fist, ready to pounce on my older brother and sock him in the eye, a loud beep came from the monitor beside CJ. Then a few other squiggly lines popped up. A nurse came into the room and her poker face was strong; I couldn't tell if this was a good thing or a bad thing. She looked over at us and smiled as she read the sheets that had printed from the monitor.

"Well, this is a great sign."

"What?" I asked the nurse, who looked old enough to be my mom. With graying hair slicked back into a ponytail and crow's feet in the corners of her eyes.

"His brain activity has gone up. What were you two doing?"

"Arguing," Ambrose answered.

"Well, he's reacting to whatever you two are saying, so that's good, but if you're arguing about him I'd suggest you stop because he can hear you."

"Do you really think so?" Ambrose looked at the nurse, genuinely concerned.

"I know so."

I walked over to CJ and placed a kiss on his cheek. "I'm sorry, but you know I'd never leave you. I don't care what he says. And when you do wake up, I hope you kick his ass."

"In his dreams." Ambrose smiled. "Well, I'm going to head out; I have to meet with Jerry in the morning to renegotiate our contracts, since CJ is still in this state."

"What are you going to do?"

"I don't know yet, but don't worry. Spasm has five members and we will not abandon our brother."

"You'd better not."

Chapter 43

Darkness is surrounding me, and I can't open my eyes. I can hear voices, but can't understand what is being said. It feels like my body is constantly falling, but there's nowhere to land.

Shadows appear behind flashes of white lights, pointing at me, guiding me away from them. *What the hell does this mean?* I feel like I'm floating outside of my own body, hovering in some type of space; a black hole. It'd felt like I'd been stuck here for an eternity.

Suddenly a jolt went through me and it felt like an elephant was sitting on my chest, I tried to inhale a deep breath and my eyes popped open. "Whe—" *Why can't I say anything out loud? What the hell is going on with me?*

I look around and the shadows had gone. I saw Shannon asleep on a small couch bed and I tried to call her name, but I couldn't. She looked terrible, and I quickly realized where I was—in some sort of hospital. My body shuddered and it felt like flames were igniting under my skin. The room was shaking and the walls were crumbling all around me. I saw a few flashes of light come by me and then darkness once again swallowed me whole.

Faint sounds were buzzing in my ear. It felt like they were getting louder and louder, but it was inaudible.

"C. . . ."

"Pla . . ."

"CJ, please. Come back to me," someone cried. It echoed in my ears, and repeatedly went through them. The voice was soft, almost angelic, but hurt. They were hurting. The shadows reappeared and I was back in the real world again.

I opened my eyes and blinked around, but I couldn't move my body. Shannon was by my side and I could see her hand on my arm, but it hurt. It felt like her skin was fusing into mine.

"CJ? Oh my God, you're awake!"

She touched my face, and tears were falling onto my chest. A loud screech boomed in my head and the darkness returned.

Chapter 44

I'd watched him carefully as his body seized. The nurses sprung into action quickly injecting something into his IV and his body finally calmed down. It looked like he was in a lot of pain and it made me feel so bad. I wish I could understand what was going on. I'd never seen anyone go through this before, but it being him, I almost wished we could trade places. I wish he didn't have to hurt or suffer anymore.

The nurses told me he was trying to come out of the coma, but something was preventing him from fully awakening. It was like he was stuck in some kind of weird limbo per se. It would explain why the second time he looked at me, he kind of freaked out, before his body seized again. His brain activity was through the roof and I was determined to help him wake up, no matter how many days I had to sit by his side.

"Ms. Moore, can I speak with you?"

"Sure, and you are?"

"Dr. Basmati. I'm overseeing Mr. Jamison's treatment and progress. I understand you two are very close?"

"Yes, I guess you could say that."

"That's fine, I know you are not married, but since we cannot get in touch with his family, I wanted to speak to you about an experimental treatment."

"What is it?"

"It's something that will help him wake up, but since he's

been in a coma for a few weeks, it'll take him a longer time to recover. He'll need a lot of physical therapy if there isn't any significant damage to his brain. We've been able to control the swelling and fluid buildup, but we won't know how bad things are until he is fully awake and functioning."

"Okay, so what do you need me to do?"

"I need consent to give him the drug. It's called zolpidem and it has worked on a few patients, some recovered remarkably, while others had no change. Since he is showing active brain waves, and is slipping in and out of consciousness, I believe he's a great candidate for the trial."

"What are the side effects?"

"Well, he could die, but that could also happen without the medicine. He could get worse, but that also could happen without treatment. It's a hypnotic sedative, but for some reason, it seems to help some coma patients wake up."

"I see, and do you really think this will help him?"

"I hope so, but it's up to you to decide if we can try it out." The doctor who looked a lot like Hugh Laurie from House, but friendlier and with fewer forehead wrinkles, handed me a clipboard with a sheet attached. The words *death* jumped off the sheet and I freaked out.

How will I be able to live with myself if this kills him? How will I be able to live with myself if I prevent them from trying?

After careful consideration and hours of web searches, I'd decided to let the doctor try the medicine. I'd rather chance him coming back, instead of being stuck in limbo with only occasional flashes of agony.

I lay in bed wide awake, staring at the lights on the ceiling, hoping this new treatment they'd start the next day would do him good. I hated the responsibility of his fate being in my hands, but I've always believed things happen for a reason.

I'd been so wrapped up with CJ that I'd forgotten all about the journalism assignment and my grades. There was a ping on my cell phone, and when I checked my email I almost hit the ceiling.

> *Dear Shannon,*
>
> *That article you submitted was pure perfection. Quite impressive. I'll get in touch with my contacts at Crush magazine and send you that letter of recommendation that you so deserve. That was a very bold choice, using an up-and-coming band and their potential rise to stardom. Most magazine companies gobble that all up, especially if they don't have to pay millions for it. I could tell by some of the wording in the article that you have a love interest in the band. If this goes public you need to make sure you're protected — if it's a bother for you. I hope to see you back in class next semester.*
>
> *Great job, Ms. Moore.*
>
> *Warm regards,*
>
> *-Professor Williams*

Oh my God, could this be real life? Maybe the stars were finally aligning for me and I'd catch a break. But as happy as I'd been about my grades, I couldn't imagine all this success without CJ being a part of it.

Me: Pen, I did it!

Pen: What?

Me: The article? Remember? I'm getting my letter of recommendation!

Pen: Holy shit balls! Congrats, girl. We'll celebrate tomorrow!

Me: I can't, CJ starts his new treatment.

Pen: Shannon Marie Moore, you're going out. CJ is a tough son of a bitch, and he'll be fine.

Me: I hope so, Pen, I really hope so.

The music was electric, the atmosphere was calm, but my head just wasn't in it. I should be happy. I should be celebrating. That email was the best response I could have asked for. It was a step in the right direction, the direction of my future. But I couldn't be happy, knowing CJ was all alone in that hospital bed, being pumped full of a drug that could potentially take his last breath.

"Shannon, drink this." Penelope slid over a shot glass and I quickly chugged it back. Expecting some type of sweet or burning liquor, it wasn't either.

"What the heck? Is this water?"

"Yep. I can't have you completely hammered when you go back to play watchdog over your boy toy." She smiled, sliding over another shot.

Ouch. I knew that was too good to be true.

Chapter 45

Ouch! My eyes sprung open, a tingling sensation crawling throughout every joint in my body. I blinked my eyes to adjust to the blinding light surrounding me.

I woke up.

I actually woke up.

I'd finally escaped the darkness that had held me hostage. I had vivid memories of slipping in and out of consciousness, but that's it. I don't know how long I've been here; I don't know what the hell happened—nothing. I wanted to see Shannon, but she wasn't here. No one was here. Why was I all by myself with these rats in lab coats?

"Nurse, he's awake! Mr. Jamison, is there anything you'd like? I know you're probably scared and confused, but everything will be all right, I assure you. I am Dr. Basmati and I've been overseeing your treatment."

There were a lot of things I wanted to say, but whatever it was that connected my thoughts to my mouth was fucking broken. My mouth was dry, my lips were chapped, and the muscles in my arms were barely there. *What in the fuck happened to me? And how long had I been here?*

"Sha—"

"Excuse me?"

"Sha—"

"Sha? Oh, you want the girl that's been here with you?

Shannon?"

I tried to move my head, but it hurt. I blinked my eyes twice, hoping this guy got the reference.

"I'll give her a call. She's barely left your side; she was practically forced by someone to take a break."

The guy in white was mumbling something irrelevant. I didn't care about any of that. I wanted her now and he needed to go and fucking get her.

Every time I tried to move it hurt. My legs, feet, toes—it all hurt. *What kind of hell is this?*

At some point I'd stopped fighting with my body and succumbed to the tingling. I must have gone back to sleep because I had the worst nightmare imaginable. I dreamt that the mob had shot me—wait, they did fucking shoot me. I remember now. The performance, the room, they were in there and fucking shot me. *But what happened to them? Fuck, where was Rico? Did anyone else get hurt?*

"CJ?" I heard faintly, tearing me away from the fucked-up thoughts running rampant through my mind. I looked up and there she was. My angel. She was wearing a long white top, her hair was in a clump on top of her head and her eyes were bloodshot.

"Sha—"

"It's okay, CJ. You don't have to speak, I'm just glad you're finally awake. I'm glad you're back and can see me. You gave me quite the scare. I thought I'd never see your beautiful eyes ever again." She placed her hand on my arm, but I couldn't feel her touch.

Chapter 46

I slept like crap the night before. I wanted to be at the hospital with CJ, but Penelope convinced me to take the night off. I knew she meant well, but I should have stayed. I wanted to see for myself if the drugs worked.

As I lay on my couch, eyes burning from the tears I couldn't quit shedding, my phone buzzed on the coffee table. I picked it up and saw *St. Francis* flash across the screen. *Oh my God, what if it killed him?*

"H-hello?"

"Shannon?"

"Speaking."

"Hi, this is Nurse Rubia calling from St. Francis Hospital. Your friend Mr. Jamison is awake and looking for you."

The words caught in my throat. Tears of joy slid down my cheeks. I swallowed hard and told her, "I'm on my way." I didn't care if I smelled. I didn't care what I looked like. Cody Jamison was awake and that was the best thing I could ever hope for. I tossed my stringy, unwashed hair into a messy bun on the top of my head and ran out the door with my white nightgown on, grabbing my purse, and a coat.

The closer I got to his room, the harder my heart pounded. Between the drive and the elevator ride to his floor, I felt like I couldn't get there fast enough. I peered around the doorframe and he was lying there, awake and alert. Quite different from what I'd seen previously.

When our eyes connected, I felt it. The electricity pulling me toward him made my knees shake from the anticipation. I just wanted to jump in the bed and hold him close. Let him feel my skin near his. Remind him of the bond we'd had since childhood.

He tried to speak, but I could tell it was a challenge. I told him not to, because I knew it would take time to get back to where he once was. I grabbed a chair and sat beside him, rubbing his arm as he stared at me. Studying me, as if I were a quiz he wanted to ace.

The doctor had come in and wanted to examine CJ. CJ's nostrils flared and he tried to move his arms, but couldn't. I could tell he didn't want our reunion to be interrupted so quickly.

"Doc, could you give us a moment? I just got here and—"

He glanced at us, and gave me a nod. "Sure, I'll be back in twenty minutes to talk about phase two of his treatment."

"I know you're wondering what he's talking about. That guy right there may have saved your life, CJ. I don't know if you would have come out of the coma if he hadn't told me about this experimental drug. But, it worked and I'm so glad."

He rapidly blinked his eyes, and tried to say something else, but it was like he was thinking so hard and the words wouldn't form in his mouth. It was sad to see, but I rather see him like this and work on getting better, than to not seeing him move at all.

I pressed my lips against his cheek. The stubble that was left after my brother had trimmed his beard tickled my lips, but I did it again.

I spent the majority of my visit explaining to CJ what happened. I didn't bring up the mob or any of that stuff, because be it as it may, I didn't feel safe talking about that in the hospital. I told him about me staying at the hospital all the time, ignoring everyone just to be by his side. A few tears escaped from his eyes, and I didn't know if they were happy or sad. What mattered the most was that there was a possibility for him to get better.

"Mr. Jamison, now this drug we'll start you off on will be a low dose at night and in the morning we'll send you to physical therapy. We've got to get you up and walking again. Your most recent MRI shows very minimal damage to your brain, so I think your speech will return back to normal very soon. We'll also have a speech therapist on hand to assist you."

"You hear that, CJ? You'll definitely get back to your old self."

He looked at his hands and the frustration returned. *Crap, the guitar.* He wanted to play the guitar.

"Doc, what about playing guitar?"

"Anything is possible, but let's just take things one step at a time, and one day at a time."

"Okay."

"Ms. Moore, I'm going to have to ask you to leave so we can administer his medication and give him something to sleep. You're more than welcome to come back in the morning during physical therapy."

"Gee, thanks." I gave CJ a kiss on the lips and walked toward the door, my feet and heart heavy because I had to leave so soon. "I'll be back as soon as I can, CJ."

As I walked through the halls of the hospital, I realized something major had happened. There were doctors and nurses running everywhere. Ambulances pulling up, but I was too distracted in my thoughts of CJ to care. As I made it to the garage and got into my car, the tears flowed. I couldn't see, I couldn't stop, I had no idea what came over me. *Was it relief washing over me? I'll never know.*

Chapter 47

After a few weeks of the physical therapist pushing me harder than I'd ever been pushed in my fucking life, I was finally able to grasp a rubber ball in my hand without shaking or dropping it. I was able to move my head and neck without any pain and the dosage of that experimental medicine had been significantly decreased. I'd made Shannon go home because it didn't make any sense for her to be here all the time.

She texted me all day and I laughed because I had to voice text her back and the auto correct was fucking hilarious.

I only needed the speech therapist for about a week or so before I could talk normally again. He'd told me it was like a switch was turned off inside my brain for a while, and it was taking a bit to reboot again. But once it did, thank fuck, I didn't want to shut up.

Jerry and the band had wanted to come and visit me, and although I know they'd seen me at my worst, I wasn't ready to face them yet. If I faced them, I'd have to explain shit and I wasn't ready for that. I couldn't let them know the truth, not until I was back on my own two feet. Not until I was me again, and not a shell of my former self.

Since I'd been confined inside these four walls for so long, I'd started to get stir crazy. I wanted to get back to my former life. I wanted to make music and rock out with the band. When Shan told me they postponed our tour and shit, I was livid. I couldn't let her know that, but I felt like a piece of shit. I felt like I was the scum of the earth for putting their dreams on hold because of a stupid debt I shouldn't have had to carry in the fucking first place.

I still had a hard time holding a pen steady in my hand, but I was determined to get these words in my head down on paper somehow. My brain was ready to get back to work, even if my body wasn't quite up to speed yet.

"Shannon, bring me my guitar. I've got magic to create."

Shannon: *You got it babe.*

The plus side to being in here was that nothing could distract me once the lyrics started flowing.

Tattered Love
Oooo, yeah, tattered love
Oooo, yeah, tattered love
Our love is a tattered one
One that should not be undone
Your smile, your touch
I'd embraced them so much
Why did you leave me this way?

This shit is gonna be good.

"Mr. Jamison, you've improved quite a bit in these few weeks. Your motor skills are getting stronger, and your speech is immaculate. You should be able to go home within a few weeks. We'll be transferring you to a rehab facility, and then once you're at about seventy-five percent, you'll be released and free to go home."

"Are you serious? Why can't I just go home and then come back here to see the physical therapist?"

"I wish it were that easy, but you have to be monitored as

you're being weaned off of the medicine. You haven't encountered any side effects yet, but that doesn't mean things couldn't get worse. It doesn't mean that once this medicine isn't flowing through your system any longer, that you couldn't possibly fall back into a coma."

"Great, just what I needed to fucking hear."

Fuck this medicine, and fuck rehab.

Chapter 48

"How do I look?" I asked Penelope as I smoothed my hands over the navy blue pencil skirt and white blouse I was wearing.

"Like you're going to nail this fucking interview."

"I hope so. Landing this job would mean the world to me."

"You deserve it, and don't you let anything stop you from going for your dreams—ever. Life is way too short not to excel at any crazy idea that little brain of yours can hatch!"

Most of the time Penelope busted my chops, but this time I could tell she was proud of me. She knew how much I'd stressed myself out worrying about CJ.

"Ms. Moore, your article was quite impressive. It was almost like you predicted the future. I've heard fantastic things about this group, Spasm. They have quite the following on YouTube and other social media outlets. Your grammar is also immaculate, and so is your proofreading."

"Thank you so much. I guess I did have a feeling that they'd skyrocket to the top. And I take great pride in my work; I'll edit and re-read until my eyes bleed."

"Wonderful. Now, tell me. Why do you want to be a journalist?" Mr. Winston was very intimidating, even when he tried not to be. With his salt and pepper hair coating his head and face, his tailored suit fit him nicely in places I hadn't expected to gaze at.

"Because I love to write. I love to be in the now, living raw and uncut. I love to feel things and pour my thoughts out on paper, bleeding the love and dedication the story deserves."

"Okay, tell me about yourself in under two minutes."

"I actually like to study; I'm a nerd and live for reading. I'm a homebody, but I've been known to shake my butt on occasion." He covered his mouth with his hand and laughed, a deep belly laugh, one that shattered the barrier and went through your core.

"Continue."

"I love Co—"

"Ah hah! There it is. The vulnerability. All journalists need to have that trait, but you need to know when to keep it under wraps. I like you, Shannon. I think you'd make a fine addition to the Crush magazine family. I need to look at your portfolio, and we can talk a little further about your career. Leave your folder there and I'll get back to you within the hour. Feel free to take a look around. My assistant, Cherry, will be more than happy to take you on a tour. Cherry, please escort Ms. Moore around the facility please," he said, pushing and then releasing the small button on his personal desk intercom.

"Thank you so much!" I said, as I exited his small, bland office.

Cherry met me in the hallway and she was absolutely gorgeous. Her hair was bright red, the asymmetrical dress she wore accented and complimented every curve on her body. Her shoes were awesome and there was no way I could wear a spiked heel, but she was able to pull it off flawlessly.

"So, let's get this tour going, shall we? And just to let you know, you've already gotten the position."

"Ho-how do you know?"

"Because I've been here for four years, and he's only sent two people on tour."

"Really, who?"

"You and me." She laughed.

"Wow, I feel honored."

"As long as you're not here for my job, you will be honored," she deadpanned. "Lighten up, I'm kidding. You'll need to develop a backbone and thick skin really quickly in here. You'll be antagonized a lot."

I was born for this job.

Cherry showed me around the entire suite, then throughout the whole building. There was a lot to see, and a lot to learn. I had no idea how she kept up with every single department. She brought me to the design room and I got to physically watch as they laid the aluminum plates down on this huge conveyer belt and the paper spun through the machine to color it and add the ink. I even got to test out one of the printers and design a mock magazine cover. It was an amazing experience. I felt like I was with her for more than an hour, but Mr. Winston eventually called us back to his office and hired me on the spot. He told me I could start immediately.

> **Me:** I got the internship!
>
> **Pen:** Bitchin,' I knew you would! Don't forget to blow the boss so you'll get paid faster.
>
> **Me:** OMG, Pen, stop that!
>
> **Pen:** :D

I'd wanted to text CJ, but I knew he had his first day at the rehab center and I didn't want to bother him. We could celebrate later.

Chapter 49

"What are your goals here, Mr. Jamison?"

"Are you kidding me? My *goal* is to get my fucking hand coordination back so I can play the damn guitar again. My *goal* is to be able to beat off without my hand cramping the hell up. Is that enough *goals* for you, Chad?"

"That's a start. So you're a musician, let's start with this." He clenched his hand together in a tight ball for a few seconds then reopened his hand, fingers spread.

"Seriously?"

"Yes, it's not as easy as it may seem."

I closed my hand, but I couldn't clench it together as tightly as he did and it pissed me off. I opened my hand and then flipped him the middle finger.

"Keep at it, you'll get stronger. Try this one." He placed his hand down flat on a table beside me, stretching his fingers, for about twenty seconds and then relaxed them. "Try this four times on each hand."

I copied him on my left hand, but my right hand wouldn't cooperate at all. "What the hell, man!" I yelled as I slammed my fist down on the table.

"It's all right, if you keep practicing these every day, you'll be playing the open E and A power chord in no time."

Wow, he actually knew some guitar lingo. I may have to give this man some credit. "Okay, Chad. I'll keep doing your little exercises and I better be able to play some Led Zeppelin by the end of my stay."

"You will, I guarantee it. I have one more exercise I want you to try." He held his hand out in front of him, palm facing toward him and bent his fingers in and down. "Try not to stress your fingers too much, while you bend. You should feel the base of each joint, making a claw shape with your hand."

"Got it!"

"I'll be back to check on you in a few minutes."

As much as I hated to do these exercises, I needed to get my hand strength and coordination back. I'll never take any of those gifts for granted ever again if I get them all back.

After my session, my hands hurt a lot, but the pain was worth it. When I was wheeled back into my room, I immediately texted Shannon. I knew she had her interview today and I hoped to hear some good news.

Me: You've been quiet, what happened?

Shannon: It was great, I got the position!

Me: That's great.

Shannon: How was rehab?

Me: Sucked balls, but it'll be worth it to get back to normal.

Shannon: You will and then you'll get out of prison.

Me: I missed you.

Shannon: I missed you too.

Me: Once I get out of hell, I'll make it up to you.

Shannon: I can't wait. Now go and get some rest.

Chapter 50

Rehab had been going great and with hard work, I was finally able to hold a guitar and strum it with my right hand. It was one of those toy ones, but fuck, it was better than nothing.

"Good morning, Mr. Jamison."

"Chad, it's Cody, you're making me feel old as fuck when you call me that."

"Sorry. I brought you something new to play with today." He placed a guitar case next to me, and pulled out an old school Gibson.

"Holy shit, I haven't seen one of these in forever."

"It's my dad's. Once you're done with your rehab stint, you can have it."

"Really? What about your dad?"

"He's dead, and it's just been collecting dust in the attic."

"Wow, thanks, dude. You don't play at all?"

"Don't mention it. And sometimes, but it's not a major part of who I am." Chad was a pretty cool kid. He was about my age, with long blond hair, and he was ripped. "Now I want to see you grasp the fret in your left hand and strum with your right."

The guitar was so beautiful I almost hated to touch it. It was in mint condition, without a single scratch. The dark wood had a glossy finish to it, and the strings were thicker than the ones on my electric. I hadn't played acoustic in a while, but it felt natural once I had it in my arms.

I strummed it slowly at first, and tuned it to my liking. Then I strummed again. *Perfect.*

"Now, I want you to place your third finger on the fifth fret on the E string. Good. Now I want you to put your first finger on the third fret on the E string."

I followed along to his instructions and as I played those two chords over and over, it was starting to sound like an old Led Zeppelin song, "Misty Mountain Hop." I knew after those two chords was an open E and once I added it in, his smiled widened.

"I see what you did there, Chad."

"I told you that you'd play a Zeppelin song before you left."

"Holy shit, I'm getting out of this place?"

"In a few days. You've been here for a couple weeks and I think you're ready for the real world again."

Wow. "I feel like I just got here."

"Well, your hand coordination is getting better, you can walk with assistance from the walker, and soon I'm sure you'll be off that, but there's no reason you need to stay here. A physical therapist can come by your house and give you a few extra sessions."

"Will it be you?"

"Unfortunately, no, but they'll send you Joe. He's a hard core Metallica fan."

"Bitchin.'"

"Now keep on practicing, and I'll be back in a bit to take you to your room."

I played the chords faster and faster, giving my own little flair to it. *I get to go home soon!*

Chapter 51

"Guys, be quiet! He's almost here, my brother just texted me." CJ was finally coming home from rehab and we all wanted to surprise him when he got there. The band, a few friends from Charlemagne's, Penelope, and a few others were all crouching behind the furniture in their cramped apartment.

We heard the keys jiggle twice in the door before it opened and we all yelled surprise. The look on CJ's face was questionable. I couldn't tell if he was happy, pissed, or almost crapped himself because a group of people were screaming at him as soon as he hit the doorway. Either way, he looked good. He looked stronger, he was still using a walker for assistance, but he almost looked like the old CJ. *My CJ.*

I let the band attack first and patiently waited behind the futon. I'd seen him more often than they had, and when it was my turn, I wasn't going to hold anything back.

Once our eyes connected, I felt like the sea of people parted and it was just us in the room. He pushed his walker aside and moved slowly over to me. Once he was near, he gave me the biggest hug. He whispered in my ear, and just the slightest touch from his lips set fire to my body. "Later, me and you, your place, and I don't give a fuck who knows."

I snapped my head back and his eyes darkened. I knew he meant business and I wasn't going to stop him from getting what he wanted. We pressed our lips together in a sweet harmony. There were gasps, claps, and other noises, but I didn't care.

"I love you, CJ."

"I love you too, Shan."

"Now go and mingle with your friends before they try and stab me in the back."

"No one's gonna off you or get off on you, but me!" He laughed. A sweet sound I'd missed so much.

It was the middle of the night and everyone was still hanging out, drinking, and catching up with CJ. Penelope kept trying to talk to Reg, but he was being weird again. I hated how on and off he was with her. She looked like she was trying to tell him something important, but he was too out of it to pay attention. *Dick.*

I was sitting on the futon, nursing a beer and listening to some soft rock in the background, when Penelope rushed over to me, dark streaks from her mascara running down her face. I knew I had to get her out of there.

"Don't say a word, let's go." I grabbed her hand, and rushed past everyone. I looked over at CJ and mouthed that I'd call him later. He looked concerned, but now wasn't the time for small talk. My best friend was hurting and I needed to get her some ice cream and let her ugly cry it out.

We ran out the door and hopped right into my car.

"Shan, wait. I've got to tell you something."

"It can't wait until we're back at my place?"

"No, I need to tell you now."

"Okay." She looked at me with fresh tears sliding down her face. "I'm pregnant."

Chapter 52

After Shannon and her friend bailed, I wasn't really interested in partying with anyone anymore. "Hey, Dean?"

"Yeah, buddy?"

"I'm getting tired."

"All right, everyone. The man of honor is tired, so it's time for you to get your shit and go. As the song goes, 'You don't have to go home, but you can't stay here.'" Everyone grabbed their stuff and headed out the door, making sure to say goodbye to me as they left.

Damn, this dude really knows how to clear a room.

"Thanks, bro. I'm gonna shower and take my rightful spot on the couch."

"Nah, not tonight, bro. You can stay in my room."

"No, man, it's not necessary."

"It's cool, my room's closer to the bathroom than yours. Besides, I'm lucky you're still here to use my room, so don't argue and just take it. You can pay me back later."

As I hobbled down the hallway and into my room for a change of clothes, I felt off. I felt like I shouldn't be here. I felt like I didn't deserve to be here. I grabbed a tank and some basketball shorts and hobbled back across the hall to the bathroom. Since I'd gotten hurt, I avoided looking at myself in the mirror. I was in denial about the scarring that was left on my body. I could feel it, but I never really sat there and looked at the damage that had been done to me.

I stepped in front of the mirror and what I saw staring back wasn't me. I still had some bandaging around my ribs from the bullets being removed. My hair was a few inches long, but I could feel the scars underneath. I had dark circles around my eyes, and looked an overall hot mess. It was hard to sleep, not knowing if I had to watch my own back or not. I never knew what happened to the hitmen. If they found out I wasn't dead, I was sure they'd come back to finish the job. *Like they finished off my family.*

Grabbing a pair of scissors, I cut the bandaging off and looked at the three holes penetrating my skin. One under my heart, one just above my navel, and the other in my lower abdomen; the areas were still sore, so I didn't touch them too much. *Fuck.*

I pulled out a pair of clippers and trimmed the thick beard off my face before stepping into the hot shower. I needed to wash the smell of rehab off of me.

After a thorough scrubbing, and a decent shave to my face, I got dressed, climbed into Dean's bed and let the darkness consume me.

Chapter 53

"I know," I said, as I stuck the key into the ignition.

"I fucked up, Shan. At first, I thought I was just coming down with something, the flu; hand, foot, and mouth—anything would have been better than this."

"Does he know?"

"Who knows! I kept trying to talk to him tonight, but he was so out of it that he just kept walking away from me, acting as if I wasn't there."

"I hate that man so much!"

"Me too, a part of me wants to keep the baby out of spite. But the other part of me wants to get rid of it, because I don't think I can handle bringing something this precious into the world with such a piece of shit attached to its bloodline."

"Ultimately it's your decision, whether he's in the kid's life or not. But just make sure you do what's best for you. Either way, I'm here as your support."

"I know, and that's why I love you. Maybe we could raise it together, be like sister-moms or some shit."

"No you did not just say sister-moms! What am I gonna do with you?" I cackled.

"Nothing, you're stuck with me for life! I am hungry though. Can we go and get some chicken?"

"I thought you'd never ask."

After our chicken excursion, I dropped Penelope off and

made it back home at some ungodly hour in the morning. I went inside my apartment and crashed on the first soft surface I made contact with.

When I awoke the next morning, all I could think about was CJ. We never got to experience us that night. We never got to sit and talk. For weeks I'd done all the talking, but I had no idea if he could hear me. I confessed my truths, my passions, my fears, my feelings. I don't know if he knew, but he was going to know soon.

My phone rang, snapping me out of my thoughts. Penelope's face flashed across my screen. "What's up, girl?"

"Shan, something's wrong! I woke up covered in blood. I think I might be losing the baby."

"Shit, what do we do?"

"Can you come and take me to the hospital? I don't want to show up in an ambulance like some scared punk."

"I'll be right there!"

I barely recall anything after that phone call. One minute I was on the couch and the next Penelope was being wheeled into the emergency room.

After what felt like an eternity, the nurses finally let me go back to Pen's room. She had been so pale. I'd never seen her skin that milky-white before. The nurse informed me that she'd lost a lot of blood and had, in fact, lost a baby, but there was another heartbeat and it was strong.

"Holy crap, she was carrying twins?"

"Yes, she's about twenty-two weeks along, based on the ultrasound."

"Will this one be okay?"

"For now, she'll have to seek follow-up care with her obstetrician and they may put her on modified bed rest until this baby gets stronger."

"Wow, okay, thank you. Will she be awake soon?"

"She should, but she did lose a lot of blood. We had to give her two blood transfusions, so she may not wake until much later. I assure you she'll be just fine. So if you need to leave and come back that would be fine."

Dear life, can we stop putting the people I love in hospitals? I've hit my quota for the year!

"Okay."

"Would you like to see the ultrasound?"

"Sure." She handed me a small black and white photo of a white blob with arms and legs in the middle of a black space. "Is that the baby?"

"It sure is, would you like to know the sex?

"No. I want her to know first."

Seeing this helpless being, knowing it was inside my best friend, was an awesome and scary feeling. Scarier for her, I'm sure. But being on this side of things, it was just as scary. I'd be the one that would have to help her, along with juggling my own life, because she didn't have anyone. It had always been us and I couldn't break that bond now. No matter how tough things get. I love this girl like a sister.

I placed my hand on hers and then felt her stomach with my other hand. I knew nothing would happen, but it was still a surreal feeling to know that at one point there were two babies in there.

I decided to spend the night with Pen in the hospital. She'd been asleep for a long time, but I didn't want her to wake up and feel like she was alone. If I could sit in the hospital with CJ for weeks at a time, a night or two here would be a walk in the park.

Chapter 54

"Hey, CJ?"

"Yeah, bro?"

"So, I know it might be soon, but me and the others were wondering what the hell happened to you?"

Shit, I was afraid of this.

"I promise, when I'm feeling up to it, I'll fill you all in."

"All right. Another question, how's your hand coordination now?"

"It's getting better, but not good enough to use a guitar all the time like I had been. I can play a few bars, a few riffs, strum a bit, but then I get tired."

"Damn, okay. Well, get some rest. I left you some coffee on the island. I've got a meeting with Jerry."

"About what?"

"About the future of Spasm."

"Is he trying to bail on us?"

"No, but he put everything on hold because of you, and now that you're back, he's going to want to proceed with things again. But, I need to let him know that just because you came home, doesn't mean you're ready yet."

"I see, well, let me know what he says. The physical therapist is coming over soon and I need to get my ass out of bed, so I can get to work."

"Sounds good, bro. Don't push yourself too hard, I need you at one hundred percent, not fifty."

"You got it."

After he left, I checked my phone and hadn't had any messages from Shannon. I hoped nothing bad happened with her and her little girlfriend. I had a sneaking suspicion Reg fucked up, but that was nothing new, he always did that.

> **Me:** Hope everything is okay, I'll be cashing in that IOU very soon, Ms. Moore.

> **Shannon:** Yeah, girl stuff. And I can't wait!

The physical therapist came and went and I hadn't gotten as tired with him as I had with Chad. Hopefully I wouldn't need too many more sessions to ditch the walker and clutch the guitar in my hands like I used to. He worked me from head to toe, and I decided to stay off the walker for a little while to see if I could stabilize my body.

Dean returned home, and he didn't look happy at all. Whenever he came home and cracked open a beer, I knew nothing good was coming out of his mouth next.

"All right, lay it on me. Am I kicked out of the group?"

"Not quite."

"What happened?"

"He told me you had four weeks to get yourself back in shape, or we'd have to find a replacement lead guitarist."

"And you told him to fuck off, right?" He wouldn't look at me. He slid his dark hair back on his head with his hand and grasped the beer can tighter. "Dean? Don't tell me you're really considering replacing me?"

"You wouldn't be replaced. You could still sing and write songs, you just wouldn't play."

"You just wouldn't play." Hearing those four words shook me. I wasn't me without having a guitar strapped to my back. I couldn't just be a puppet for them to use, while some half-rate stand-in was getting all the credit. *Fuck that.* I had major work to do and in four short weeks, I was gonna be the new and improved version of myself, so help me God.

After the first week of in-home physical therapy and pushing myself, I was in so much damn pain. The next few days became a blur, due to heavy pain meds, but before I knew it, I didn't need my walker anymore. I could walk in straight lines, stand from a sitting and kneeling position.

One more week and I'll be able to tell Jerry to suck my balls. I'm back, bitch!

Chapter 55

"I've called you all to my office to renegotiate your contract and to see how we will proceed with the tour that had been canceled per your request. Cody, I'm glad to see you back, but are you sure you're ready for this?"

"As ready as can be expected. I'm not gonna sit here and lie to you, Jerry. I get tired sometimes, and other times I'm fine. My hands cooperate most times, and occasionally they do whatever the fuck they want, but this is my livelihood, my fucking dream. No second-rate stand-in is gonna pose as the lead guitarist while I sit on the sidelines like a little bitch, harmonizing with Red. No offense, Red."

"None taken. Feel free to speak your mind, I kind of like it."

"I just can't let that happen. This band is my family and we'll play together until we're all dead."

"So, do you all agree with this?"

"Hell yeah, Spasm isn't Spasm without our resident spazz-ass," Dean said.

"All right, well, the contract remains the same. You'll stay with me for one year, you'll start off touring locally, and then you'll do a three-month tour across the country. You think you guys are ready for that?"

"Damn right!" we all said simultaneously.

"Now get your asses back in the studio and create me another number one hit single!"

We all grabbed our things and went across the hall to the full studio. There was no engineer in there, which was perfect; we needed to talk and brainstorm before we made music. We always came up with a few bars and melodies fairly quickly, so there wasn't much to worry about—except the fact that I have to tell them what the hell happened before they start to interrogate me.

As soon as we all took a seat on the long leather couch, everyone looked over at me. I knew then, that it was now or fucking never.

"All right, let's address the elephant in the room. I'm originally from Canada, my family moved here when I was a baby. My dad is a jackass that likes to gamble, and he got into some trouble with the mob, forcing us to move. The debt was then passed on to me, because he'd gotten sick and couldn't afford to pay his debt. I couldn't live with myself hurting and stealing from innocent people, so my friend and I stopped paying our debts and fled the country. As you can tell, they wanted me dead, but didn't succeed. Now can we rock now or what?"

"Holy fuck, dude. They're not, like, coming back, are they?" Colt asked.

"I doubt it, and if they do I doubt that you guys are in any danger. If you were, you wouldn't be here right now."

"That's good enough for me," Reg said. "My life's already fucked, and I'm sure I've got some assholes who want my head on a stake."

"What the fuck, CJ! There are henchmen out there that will probably come back and try to kill us all because you didn't die!" Dean shouted.

"I don't think that'll happen."

"But how the fuck do you know? And what about my sister? What if those assholes come back and kill her instead? You know, to make you pay for fucking them over. How am I supposed to live like that, knowing she could be in constant danger?"

Holy shit, I hadn't expected him to respond like that, but I couldn't blame him. All of this was scary and you never know when your life could be over.

"We were always in constant danger, yet every single one of us is still here. If you want me to go, Dean, I will, but know this, I will not come back. So y'all need to get together and make a fucking decision now. We either deal with it as a fucking family or I walk and you can explain to Shannon why I left."

I stormed out of the studio and booked it straight for the elevators. *I can't believe this shit.*

Before I made it out the front door, they all came running behind me off of the second elevator. "CJ, wait!" Alexis shouted.

"What?"

"Where the fuck do you think you're going?" Reg asked.

"I was going for a walk, didn't know how long it'd take for you guys to figure this shit out."

"There wasn't anything to figure out. We told Ambrose to calm the fuck down and we'll feel things out. We almost lost you once, there is no fucking way we're going to lose you again," Colt said.

"Now bring your dusty ass back upstairs and write us another hit single," a deep voice commanded from down the hall.

"Dean, you sure? There's still time to say no."

"We're good, you know how I get when it comes to my sister. We'll figure it out. Life is too short for the what-ifs, and I'm pretty sure she'd never forgive me if you left, anyway."

Holding the guitar for long periods of time started to wear on my hands and arms. I didn't want to say anything and bitch out like a little pussy, but Dean could tell I was starting to hurt. "All right, guys, let's give this a rest. He looks good, but we don't want to physically push this guy too much. We need him at one hundred percent on tour, not twenty."

"Good, because I'm tired as hell," Colt said. "I needed a nap like three hours ago."

"Damn, have you all gotten soft while I was lying on my death bed?"

"Pretty much. I was ready for the time off before we got back into this hardcore," Alexis said.

"Wow, well, I guess we all need to get our asses in gear. Spasm has got to make it to the top and nothing will ever stop us again. Do you hear me? Not a damn thing!"

We all closed up shop and locked up the studio, ready to return the next day. We went downstairs and climbed into the van and I hated to admit it, but I missed this noisy rust bucket. We were on our way to Charlemagne's and it was a much needed reunion. I hadn't had a good beer on tap in a long time, and after all the shit we went through earlier, I may need something a little stronger.

"Well, look what the cat drug in! Cody Jamison. Man, I thought you were a goner," Tom said.

"Tom, I thought I was a goner too, but it wasn't my time yet."

"I see that, good to have you back. And remember, your money's no good here, so don't even try to pay or I'll kick your ass."

"He would never!" Alexis said sarcastically, placing her hand over her heart and widening her mouth. That girl could put down a few pitchers of beer alone, and not feel a damn thing.

The bartender slid the mug down the bar, and I let it sit in front of me for a moment. I had to admire the beauty of it. Like a creep, I lifted the mug to my nose and smelled it before letting the cold draft slide down my throat, and it was the best feeling in the world. Well, second to sex. The heavy medication I was on before wouldn't allow me to drink, but I gave no fucks tonight. I was gonna party until I dropped.

I'd awoken in a strange room, a bright light flashing in my face. *No, no, please tell me I didn't fuck another random.*

My head pounded and I had no idea where I was. I saw my pants laying on the floor beside the bed and as I tried to reach for them, I fell to the floor and the world spun above my head.

"CJ, are you okay?"

"Where the hell am I?"

"You're at my place."

I swung at the voice not caring who it was, until I realized who was speaking.

"Colt? Shit, I'm sorry, dude. I'm just really confused right now. What the fuck happened last night?"

"Well," he paused, straightening his jaw. "You were drinking, and then all of a sudden you were face down at the bar. I'm going to assume that whatever you were drinking didn't mix well with the medication you've been taking. Ambrose wasn't going straight home, so Kandy and I decided to bring you here because we didn't want you to be alone."

"Okay, but why are my pants off?"

"I have no idea; they were on when you got here. Maybe you kicked them off in the middle of the night?"

"Probably, I don't like sleeping in pants."

"So, Kandy's making some breakfast, what would you like to eat?"

"I like anything that's edible and will make this ringing in my head stop."

"I'll go and grab you some aspirin and a bottle of water, but let me help you back onto the bed first."

"Thanks, man, don't tell anyone about this. I didn't mean to hit you." After he assisted me back on the bed, I felt sluggish. I felt like my body was full of cement and I could hardly move on my own. This was a new experience for me and I hated it. *Fuck.* I tried to lie back on the bed and let the darkness take me away, but it was too damn bright. Colt returned and I asked him to close the blinds so I could go back to sleep.

"Okay. Do you need anything else?"

"Yeah, come back with something hot and greasy in about an hour."

"You got it, bro. Rest up; we have practice in a few hours. And Jerry will have our balls if we don't work on that demo."

"I'll be good, I promise."

Chapter 56

"Shannon?"

"Hey, you. How are you feeling?"

"Like I've been hit by a truck, what happened?" she asked, struggling to shift her body.

"Well . . . you had a miscarriage an—"

"I lost the baby?" she interrupted.

"Yes and no."

"Shannon, what the hell? Quit fucking with me."

"You were carrying twins, and one didn't make it."

All of the color in her face had faded as she quickly tore her eyes away from mine. Placing her hand on her stomach a few tears rolled down her cheek. "There were two inside of me?"

"Yeah, here, look at this. The nurse gave me it." I handed her the black and white photo and her cheeks lit up.

"Is that my baby?"

"Yeah, your little survivor."

"I like that, my little survivor."

"They said you lost a lot of blood and had to give you two blood transfusions."

"Damn, I was on the way out."

"Basically. But someone wanted to keep you here a bit longer."

"Good, because I'd hate to miss you and CJ's wedding."

"Oh my God, no! That—I—don't."

"Aw, you hadn't planned your wedding yet? I thought all girls who were into rockers did that shit."

"Don't tell me, you planned one for you and Reg?"

"Unfortunately, but I didn't expect this to happen so soon," she said, pointing to her stomach.

Her bringing up marriage left a weird taste in my mouth. *I could barely keep him from putting his cock in other holes when he was unconscious, how could a ring lock everything down?*

"But anyway, have you talked to him lately?"

"Not really. We've sent a few texts, but I haven't seen him since the night before last."

"Go!"

"Go where?"

"Go and see him! Stop babysitting me and ignoring the real problem here."

"And what problem is that?"

"Your feelings. You guys need to sit down and sort that shit out as soon as possible, because the sexual tension and other shit can be felt by anyone who's around the two of you."

"I don't know what I'm feeling."

"Yes you do, you've never been one to ignore your gut. So take your ass home, shower, and invite him over to your place tonight. I don't care how late he shows up, but this needs to be sorted out now."

"Fine. I'll check in with you later. Let me know when the nurses say you can come home so I can come back and pick you up."

"I will. Shan, wait."

"What?"

"Thank you."

"You're welcome."

Midnight—nothing.

One in the morning—nothing.

My eyelids were getting heavy, my stomach churned, was he even coming?

Finally, just before two in the morning there was a faint tap at my front door. I had on a long t-shirt and was minutes away from drifting off to sleep. I walked to the door, carefully, one foot in front of the other, wiping the sleep out of my eyes. I wanted to build the suspense; I wanted him to see what it felt like to wait for something. I inched the door open and looked at him. His hands were weaved together on top of his head and he gave me his signature one-sided grin. "Are you going to let me in?"

"I don't know. Should I?"

"You waited this long for me, so I don't see why you'd be shy now."

I rolled my eyes and opened the door for him. "What the heck took you so long?"

He removed his vest, and sat across from me on the couch. His black shirt clinging to his slender frame. "Jerry, he just let us out about a half hour ago. I would have called, but my phone died."

"Oh, okay. Well, would you like something to drink?"

"No, I'm good. Shan, listen, we need to talk."

"I know, that's why I asked you to come over."

"Oh, so you go first."

"Well." A lump formed in my throat and I couldn't get it down. I took a sip of water to clear it, but it didn't help.

"Go on, Shan."

"Well, I just wanted to talk about us."

"What about us?"

Why was it so hard for me to talk to him face to face? It was like I knew I did something wrong and I had to confess to my parents, not knowing what consequences I'd face.

"I'll go, Shannon. I don't know what to do. I care about you a lot, hell, I've been in love with you since I was twelve, but I'm getting ready to go on tour and I don't know what will happen. I want to tell you I'll be committed to you and only you, but I don't know if I can promise you that. You have a career you're trying to build and I don't want to fuck that up. I don't want you to lose everything you've ever wanted for me."

"CJ, you're everything I've ever wanted."

Chapter 57

Shit, how do I respond to that? She's everything I've ever wanted too, but I couldn't let this thing—whatever the hell it was between us, get ruined. On the road there was so much fucking temptation, even if I didn't want it. It was all bound to go down in flames, and although shit can get out of hand, in the end was it worth it?

"Shannon, you're everything I've ever wanted, and that's why I can't do this to you. I can't lead you on anymore. I can't hurt you anymore. You sat in that hospital with me for weeks, ignoring what was important to you, I just can't—"

She kissed me. This wasn't a normal kiss; this was an undeniable force that was pulling us together. A sign, that she wasn't letting me go, even if I wanted her to.

"Stop it. Just stop, CJ. We can't control everything that happens in our lives, but we can navigate the path to our own happiness."

I sat back and looked at Shannon. I mean, really fucking looked at her. For some reason I'd forgotten she wasn't that little girl anymore. The one I used to play with every day. No, this was a woman, a woman in love with an asshole. An asshole who deserved to be alone, but she chose to give her heart to me, and now it's mine—all mine.

Her brown eyes were full of love, her long hair carefully pulled back away from her face, and the shirt she wore rode up as she rocked back and forth on the couch. I ran my hand up her thigh, her skin is warm with want. I spread her legs apart with my knee and she gasped as my fingers found their way inside her panties.

"Tell me how you want it," I growled in her ear.

"Real, raw, and unrestricted."

"I thought you'd never ask."

While I was in the hospital, I was tested and luckily STD free. There was no way in hell I'd be into foreplay tonight. I needed to feel her, her essence on my hand was enough to make my dick hard as a rock and I needed to feel her walls shift around it as I fucked her until she didn't have any voice left.

I ripped my fingers from inside of her and rubbed the head of my cock against her entrance. Pushing the head in, inch by inch, as her insides clenched around it. "Fuck, you're so tight." She tried to shift her hips to accommodate me, but I stopped her, holding her right where she was. "Don't you move, or I'll deliver pain first, pleasure later."

I held her leg over my shoulder, pumping in and out. I couldn't get enough; she was like a drug I constantly needed to hit. And she felt so fucking good when I did.

Her bottom lip curled and her body tensed, she was getting close and I could tell because she kept pushing me out. "Don't fight me, baby, let me in."

I placed my hand behind her neck, gave it a squeeze and she lost it. Her body convulsed under me and she yelled so loud I thought she'd wake the dead. "That's a good girl, now get on all fours, it's my turn."

She could barely move her legs and that made me want to pound into her even more. Once I got her turned over, all bets were off, this ass was mine, and no other man would be able to put his hand or his dick in or on her ever again.

Epilogue

"Spasm! Spasm!" I peered through the curtain. The crowd in this place had been a hell of a lot bigger than the last time we'd gotten to play here. With our tour ending and all the other bullshit we had to deal with, it felt good to be back. This place was where we all connected, and although we couldn't play here as often as we wanted, we said we'd try to play once a month after our break. Being on the road for three months put a toll on all of us, but I'd never change it. I'd go through everything all over again, just to be this happy.

We all gathered in a circle as Dean gave us a pep talk. "All right, guys, this is our home. This is the most important performance of our lives. Do you know why?"

"Why?" Colt asked.

"Because, if this had been months earlier, we wouldn't have Cody motherfuckin' Jamison to rock on stage with us. Not a day goes by that I'm not thankful as fuck that you survived, dude, we love the hell out of you."

"That's the only reason?" Reg asked sarcastically.

"Well, it's also the place we all connected and it'll probably be the place we all get buried, I'm sure, douche."

"Damn right, now, let's fuck shit up!" Alexis shouted.

Stepping onto that small stage was exhilarating. Electricity circulated through my body, forcing a deep release from my soul as I fingered the guitar I feared I'd never hold again. After being in a coma for so long, and countless hours with a physical therapist, I didn't think I'd be able to do much of shit, but I pulled through. The tour also had its challenges, but with dedication and the woman I love on my side, I felt like the king of the fucking world.

I searched the crowd and there she was, just as gorgeous as ever. The lights bounced off the diamond studs I'd given her and she gave me the sexiest smile. *I'll be tearing that shit up later.*

I've arrived . . . No, scratch that—*we* have arrived.

I briefly let go of my guitar and wrapped my hand around the microphone. I was gonna own this fucking song. It was our number one hit, and stayed in the Top 100 our entire tour. I knew for sure we'd be getting some awards and I couldn't wait to go for the Best New Artist plaque.

Tattered Love

Oooo, yeah, tattered love

Oooo, yeah, tattered love

Our love is a tattered one

One that should not be undone

Your smile, your touch

I'd embraced them so much

Why did you leave me this way?

You'd broken the rules, I'd committed to you

Please all I ask is the truth

What am I to do?

The tears I'd cried until blue

I'm escaping the truth, I can't live without you

Come on baby come back to me

Baby, I can't understand, baby, I don't understand

How you could leave me, and run off with another man

My brain's confused, I am missing you

JAMISON

Please save me from this shit storm

Oooo, yeah, tattered love
Oooo, yeah, tattered love
Our love is a tattered one
One that should not be undone

My heart beats for you
My blood runs for you
I need somebody to love, somebody to hold late at night
Reality came crashing down and I was distracted by the light
Blinded by the blanket you held across my eyes,
Shielding me from the monster you'd become
I can't understand, you gave me joy
Baby, I don't understand.
I just can't understand.
Now I need somebody to love
Somebody to love me
Get rid of this tattered love
Return my joy
The sunshine that was taken away
Please come back another day

Oooo, yeah, tattered love
Oooo, yeah, tattered love
Our love was a tattered one
One that indeed come undone
I will understand, baby, I can understand

Shannon

CJ had been on the road for months, but I was able to Facetime him whenever I wanted. We had phone sex, sent naughty texts and pictures to each other, so we both had something to look forward to once we were reconnected. I hadn't been able to see him perform as a paid superstar, but that night I was going to be front row and center at Charlemagne's.

I'd asked my boss to leave early that day so I could get to the concert on time because I knew that place was going to be packed.

Everything had been going well for me at Crush magazine, I'd decided to take part-time classes and focus on my internship. And all my cards finally fell into place for CJ and me. He remained faithful on tour and I made sure Alexis watched him for me to make sure he behaved. Cherry filled me in on a little secret and told me I was getting bumped up to a paid assistant that morning. I had a permanent smile on my face ever since. She also let me know that the next issue of Crush would be about Spasm and Cody would grace the cover.

Even though she wasn't feeling well, Pen came along with the baby. I guess things with her and Reggie were finally turning around because he reached out to her and wanted to make sure she was coming to the show so he could meet his daughter.

As we exited my car, I could see through the front door that it was packed to capacity. There was a line that wrapped around the building, but since we were both with members of the band, we were able to skip ahead, leaving tons of angry groupies and fans pissed off.

"Wow, a baby gets to go in before me?" an angry groupie

said.

We found a spot near the bar, and I looked down at baby Regina, sleeping peacefully in her car seat. She was so tiny and looked just like her mom, swaddled in the pink blanket I'd bought for her.

Looking at the stage was surreal for me. I'd seen CJ perform on it before, but now it was different. He was a bestselling musician now, and he was living his dream, which made me happier than anything.

The crowd was impatiently cheering and screaming the band's name, and I saw someone peeking through the curtains. After a few moments, they all emerged from behind the thin red material and wasted no time grabbing their instruments and adjusting their microphones.

CJ started the song off with a mellow guitar riff and Alexis came into the song with him. They were singing one of my favorite songs, "Tattered Love." CJ told me that he'd started writing it in the hospital, and it was a reminder of life for him. Singing it reminded him that he could have died, but he didn't. He was given a second chance at life and love and he wanted to let the world know through his music.

Watching him perform on stage was magical. The way his fingers slid up and down the fret was almost hypnotic. I felt like I was under his spell, along with the tons of his other fans, but these girls only fantasized about him; he was mine. He'd always been mine.

Everything he'd gone through, everything we'd gone through, was worth it. Cody Jamison was everything to me. He was the sunshine beaming after a fresh rainstorm, he was my jacket when it was cold outside, and he was my favorite place to be when my mind searched for peace. He was my *home*.

The crowd's intensity picked up when Reg hit his drum solo, and they went nuts when Colt played the keys. They were all so good together, and every time I think about them almost not making it, fresh tears sprung from my eyes because being around CJ taught me that life is never guaranteed, but love is.

His eyes connected with mine from the stage and I felt a

surge travel through my body. His stare was like a current and the electricity surged to my soul.

I love you, Cody Jamison, and I can't wait to see where life leads us next.

The End

Acknowledgements

I want to give a special shout out to my beta's you know who you are! I'm thankful for each and every one of you! You're never allowed to leave lol.

To Devon, you've been there with me through everything, keep on pushing me, and I'll push you back!

To Michelle Dare, if we didn't write, and piss and moan together every night, Jamison wouldn't have even been finished. Let's keep it going! Love you!

To Judy, thanks for catching the last minute things for me, I really appreciate it!

About the Author

Niquel is a self diagnosed coffee addict, lover of rice and beans, and chocolate—preferably not all together. She's the creator of multiple stories full of love, passion, and power. She may toss in a ghost story every once in a while.

When she's not busy taking care of her two little girls, she's writing or creating graphics. Or you can find her binge watching TV with her significant other.

Boston born and raised, she's always been a creative soul: attending multiple colleges to develop her love of the visual arts.

Niquel loves to meet new fans and she'd love to hear feedback from you. Whether it's positive or negative, your reviews help her grow as an author! You can contact her directly through any of the sites posted below.

Facebook ~ www.facebook.com/author.niquel
Twitter ~ www.twitter.com/authorniquel
Website ~ www.authorniquel.com/
Email ~ Authorniquel@aol.com
Goodreads ~ www.goodreads.com/authorniquel
Instagram ~ www.instagram.com/authorniquel
Signup for my **Newsletter**
(http://app.mailerlite.com/webforms/landing/v2u9g2)! No spam I promise.
Request to join my **Reader Group**
(www.facebook.com/groups/niquelsnymphs/)!

Other
Books by Niquel

A Forbidden Love

An Endless Love

The CEO

Good-bye, with Love

Bed of Lies Volume 1

Reginald (Spasm Rockers Book 2)

Look out for more Spasm Rockers in 2018

A Note
From the Author

If you've made it this far, thank you! This book means so much to me. I have no idea where it came from, but I'm glad I was able to get it out and share it with you! Some of the songs may have been a little dark, but they all came straight from my heart!

There will be more of the Spasm Rockers series coming in 2018 so stay tuned! If you loved this book as much as I did, please leave a review!

Bed Of Lies Volume 1 is now live! Volumes 2 and 3 are coming soon!

If you'd like to receive bonus content, make sure you sign up for my newsletter!

(https://app.mailerlite.com/webforms/landing/v2u9g2)

www.ingramcontent.com/pod-product-compliance
Lightning Source LLC
Chambersburg PA
CBHW020740250626
47155CB00003B/843